D0069612

THE GUBBINS CLUB:
THE LEGEND OF
CHARLIE'S GOLD

Melinda Taliancich Falgoust

Text Copyright © 2013
Melinda Taliancich Falgoust
All Rights Reserved
ISBN 978-1482690408

Dedicated to all those whom I call friend. You have filled the chapters of my life story so far with grand adventures...I can't wait for the sequel.

CHAPTER ONE

The Map

X marked the spot. Treasure maps just worked that way.

At least in fiction, Bernie McManus thought. Buried gold and sparkling jewels were a little harder to come by in real life. More often than not, when you followed the dusty clues of history, the "treasure" turned out to be a mouldy bit of leather from an old saddle. Or sometimes it was just a hunk of twisted, corroded metal that no longer resembled the brooch of some far gone ancestor.

4

No, the thrill of the modern treasure hunt was the puzzle, the unraveling of ancient mysteries that no one else could figure.

But this treasure hunt was different. Bernie had found the spot. Of that he was certain. He had carefully sifted through the tangled trail of hints and misdirections to finally discover the piece of weathered parchment, a forgotten pirate's map, where "X" did, in fact, mark the spot. Its faded scrawl promised it held the key to a golden secret, the resting place of nearly £5m in gold. He had feverishly followed the map's directions, ignoring its dark predictions for trespassing thieves.

Bernie wasn't afraid of long-dead buccaneers. As an archaeologist who enjoyed relative fame, you might say he made a living from the dead. So, why the sudden chill that rippled down his spine?

He wasn't alone.

He had first felt the odd, prickling sensation of being followed earlier in the day. When he'd left his flat that morning, Bernie noticed a short, lumpy man leaning against a nearby lamp post, reading the paper.

It only struck him because the paper was Chilean. Not a normal rag of the realm. Then later that day, he'd noticed the same man dressed in workman's togs at the library where he'd followed the trail. The repeated appearance of the odd little man prompted Bernie to drop his special package in the post.

It was also what left him feeling a bit skittish now. Tyrannical pirates like Black Bart and Captain Kidd may have dissolved to ash and dust years ago, but modern men existed who were just as vicious and shared no loyalty to the treasure trove laws of Scotland.

Bernie ducked down behind a sandy dune as the searching Fidra light swept toward the beach. A light breeze rustled through the tall grasses on the Yellowcraigs shore, whispering in the night. Treasure, treasure, treasure.

Bernie squinted through the dark, certain he had caught a furtive movement at the edge of his vision. He waited for the pass of the lighthouse beam once again. Suddenly, a dark shape swooped toward him.

"Ca-caw! Ca-caw!" Bernie fell over backward as a herring gull narrowly missed his head. He grinned crookedly as the bird wheeled off toward the tiny island. Probably a resident of the Seabird Centre tucking into a late night snack.

He looked out over the firth at the keyhole stone arch, the two dark humps of Fidra looking like some great sea beast slumbering in the shallows – a dragon guarding its hoard. And Bernie meant to be the one to claim it for the Crown.

He pulled his small skiff toward the lapping waves. As he reached the edge of the black water, he stepped into the tiny boat and reached for the oar. At that moment, the cold, pale light of Fidra swept over the dunes once more. Bernard McManus, a rational man of science, suddenly found his boyhood fantasies of swashbuckling, bloodthirsty pirates flooding back as the light glinted coldly off a raised hook of metal.

CHAPTER TWO

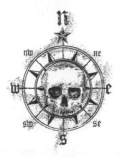

The Monkey's Fist

The parcel arrived at post, nondescript in plain brown wrapping paper, addressed to Master Colin McManus, 42 Henderson Row, Edinburgh, EH3 5 BL. At first, the postmaster thought little of it. Hundreds of parcels like this passed through his office with regularity, and he dutifully shuttled them on to schools and the like where eager students awaited the assorted sweets, the bits of licorice rope, and the buttery shortbread rounds.

On this day, however, this one package caught

the interest of the balding little postmaster. It was small and rectangular, like so many of the others, yet the hemp binding the package together was fashioned in a most peculiar knot. Being a man of letters with no nautical persuasion, the knot was truly foreign to him.

He adjusted his wire-rimmed spectacles, eyeing the knot suspiciously. A bleary blue eye roved over the intricacies and weaves. It suddenly struck the postmaster that it looked much less like a knot and more like the paw of a small animal with long, slender fingers gripping a prize. The oddity of the knot roused the curiosity of the postmaster so that he broke protocol and gave the box a gentle shake.

No ticking. No loose claptrap rattling around. Just the odd twisting of rope binding. Another boring care package.

So, with no further thought to the matter, he stamped the package with its proper postmark and rattled it along the conveyor towards Auld Reekie, Edinburgh Academy, and a small, wheezy, spectacled boy named Colin McManus.

CHAPTER THREE

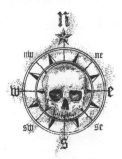

Smout

When you were small, Smout reasoned, life came at you one of several ways. Quite often, people thought you absolutely precious and your face succumbed to much cheek-pinching as your head got jollied back and forth.

If you were fortunate, people overlooked you entirely, and you remained free to go about your business, cheeks unaccosted. Of course, however, if your luck ran to the sour, as Smout's often did, you fell into the far less desirable third category – bully fodder.

He wasn't even certain into whose locker he had been stuffed. Maddagh Donaldson wasn't picky when it came to his bullying tactics. Smout's nose wrinkled at the distinct odor of dirty athletic socks, that odd corn crisp smell. He supposed it could be the locker of a member of one of the sporting teams. A cleat jabbed neatly into his bum. Yes. Definitely an athlete.

As he rubbed his backside, he squinted into the deserted corridor, the world narrowed to the three thin slats moulded into the locker door. He squirmed in the confining space, contorting like a circus acrobat, till the luminous glow on Uncle Bernie's explorer watch turned his freckle-splattered face a sea-sick green. The pale light reflected eerily off his round-framed spectacles as Smout managed a grin at his most cherished possession.

His uncle bequeathed the watch to him last year after returning from a dig in the Amazon rainforest. Uncle Bernie firmly believed the world existed to be explored and a treasure certainly hid under every rock. To solve the mystery, one simply had to interpret the clues.

"But, a proper adventurer needs proper tools!" Uncle Bernie bellowed as he slapped the over-sized watch on Smout's bony wrist. The timepiece had spun wildly, steadfastly refusing to remain to rights. That is, until Smout had borrowed one of Uncle Bernie's archaeology tools to punch a last hole in the band. Now it sat properly as Smout peered at its face.

The watch had been his father's. He had been a grand archaeologist like Uncle Bernie. Of course, such a grand man would have a grand watch and his was spectacular indeed. It had all sorts of gadgets and fancy whoziwhatsits. It could take accurate depth readings to thirty feet, had an altimeter to gauge heights to 30,000 feet, and featured a barometer function that registered changes in air pressure to help predict weather patterns.

At the moment, however, it merely glowed a pedestrian eight thirty-five. Smout sighed. Roll call. Perhaps someone would miss him and come searching.

He watched a lonely tuft of weed skitter across the empty courtyard.

"That's likely," he scoffed. "Maybe then I'll have the grandest adventure ever, discover the greatest treasure in the world and they'll crown me king of England."

He exhaled heavily and collapsed against the cold, unyielding metal.

In point of fact, most of Smout's adventures derived from incessant rounds of cribbage with Miss Dumbarton, Uncle Bernie's million-year old housekeeper. Smout swore her wrinkles had wrinkles. At any rate, best of three always turned into best of five, and so on and so forth. Cribbage wasn't her strong suit. Actually, neither was housekeeping. It wasn't unexpected to find a wedge of cheese left lingering long into the experimental science stage, or layers of dust so thick one had to employ excavation tools to locate the furniture beneath. So, while cribbage passed some of the time, Smout longed for excitement.

But real adventures beyond the walls of their

Heriot Row flat were not in the cards for Smout's frail lungs. The Edinburgh clime was not suited for someone prone to asthmatic attacks and bronchial ills. Indeed, Smout's constant battle with illness and superlative genius for running fevers left him a scrawny little whelp, a bit bug-eyed and out of the running for, well, running, or any other type of strenuous physical exertion. He frequently went to school armed with a physician's note excusing him from sports. He spent much of his life watching other children enjoy theirs.

But there were always the stories.

When Smout was quite small, Smout's mother read to him. She had been an archaeologist, too. It was a family affair. Victoria McManus, however, was small and frail, much like Smout himself. She did most of her work behind a desk. The brains behind the brawn, she'd often joke.

But in between the leather-bound pages of tall tales and grand adventures by Crusoe, Poe, Melville and Stevenson, he and his mother became great sailors and swashbuckling pirates, searching beyond the confines of Smout's small bedroom for mystery, treasure and great, white whales. His favorite...*Treasure Island.*

On one cold and rainy night, she tucked a squirming Colin into bed. It simply wasn't fair, he cried. Every kid knew parents waited until the kids were asleep to do all the really fun stuff!

His mother's laugh pealed like a clear bell. "You flop about like a young salmon on the shore! I think I'll call you Smout."

The nickname stayed, but his mother did not.

One night, while working at the National Museum of Scotland, his mother vanished, becoming much like one of the mysteries she and Smout often read. The local constabulary had no leads save for a torn half of an American dollar bill and the Latin phrase *E Pluribus Unum* scrawled on notepaper and circled in bold, red ink.

It was in the midst of this memory that a peculiar noise filtered through the narrow locker slats.

Thump. Drag. Thump. Drag. Smout cocked his head. Something familiar about the sound niggled

15

at his memory.

Thump. Drag. Thump. Drag. The sound came closer. His knee grazed his chin as he maneuvered a size four loafer into a stack of textbooks, leveraging for a better view. He had just pressed his nose against the locker grille when suddenly, his world went black.

CHAPTER FOUR

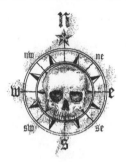

An Ill Wind

Gordon Staid liked order. The pudgy little
rector of Edinburgh Academy appreciated his daily
stroll through the Academy's halls, surveying the
students in each classroom, sitting in regimented
rows, their crisp uniform blazers a neat square of blue
in the centre of each square classroom. Each strand
of his thinning hair was carefully combed and
cemented into place over his balding pate with styling
product. And the vertical folds of his pocket kerchief
lined up with the degree of accuracy expected of a

plumb-bob.

He wiped a bit of dust from the top of his desk and promptly erupted into vicious sneezes. As his bulbous nose reddened, Staid ruminated he might, in fact, be allergic to disarray.

So, when his secretary, Dunleavey, unceremoniously slammed the news down on his neatly organized desk, and turned Staid's recently aligned row of sharpened pencils into graphite darts, the rector's cherubic cheeks flushed crimson.

"What is the meaning of this, Dunleavey!" Staid spluttered. Flecks of white spittle lodged on his lower lip. He broke into a succession of nasal explosions.

"Are you daft, man?" he accused when the attack finally subsided. Staid hefted his large frame about, scrambling to reset his desk materials to rights. The buttons on his tweed jacket strained in protest. Dunleavey paid no attention. He jabbed a long, bony finger at the headline on *The Scotsman's* front page.

"It's dreadful news, sir." Dunleavey's Adam's

apple bobbled on his long neck.

Staid perused the article to which Dunleavey so urgently alluded. "Museum curator and noted archaeologist missing!" The headline screamed in 48-point type.

"It says here it occurred on Fidra, sir," the gangly secretary offered.

The rector's brows knitted. "Not to seem callous, Dunleavey, but what does this have to do with us?"

"The Senior School expedition, sir. They had planned to travel to the Seabird Centre. On Fidra, sir. I'm afraid we'll have to cancel now."

"Tsk, tsk, tsk." Staid solemnly shook his head, his jowls waggling slightly. "This is terrible news."

Another sneeze enveloped him causing a wedge of his stiff hair to stand straight on end. He shook his head, smoothing the wayward style.

"Losing my hair, administration woes, and now this news. Things are incredibly out of sorts, Dunleavey. It's unacceptable! Unacceptable." A trio of sneezes echoed in rapid fire succession.

Dunleavey offered his employer a handkerchief.

"I'm also not quite certain what to do with this, sir." Dunleavey proffered a small package to the rector. "This came today for one of our students, sir."

The rector took the package, twirling it about in his beefy hands. He nudged his spectacles down his nose and gave the box a once-over.

"That's a bit unusual. Why would a student receive a package here?"

"I'm afraid I've no idea, sir. Note the name." Dunleavey pointed to the name which appeared to have been scrawled in great haste.

"McManus?" Staid queried.

"Yes, sir. The name of the missing archaeologist."

The two men paused for a moment to ponder the mystery. Staid handed the package back to his gangly secretary.

"Shall I pass it along, then?" Dunleavey questioned.

"Yes, yes. Of course. It belongs to the boy. Make sure that he gets it," Staid ordered, washing his hands of the matter.

Dunleavey cleared his throat. "I'm afraid there's more, sir."

Staid inhaled sharply, poised for another brain-rattling sneeze. He breathed a sigh of relief as the urge passed.

Dunleavey pulled at his collar, twisting uncomfortably. "Mr. Bluidy is in your outer office, sir."

Gordon Staid sneezed so hard, the entire cache of reorganized pencils sailed across the room once more.

Staid's blustery voice dropped to an almost imperceptible whisper. "What does he want?"

The answer was simple. An eight-letter word for portent of ill fortune? Sinister. Rory swiftly penciled in the answer.

"Take that *Scotsman*!" the teenager celebrated. Puzzles and codes fell out neatly for Rory. He supposed it was genetic. His father was a cryptographer. MI6. He spent all day cracking codes and secret messages. It was incredibly cool to have a spy as a dad, Rory supposed. Of course, he couldn't really share his day at the supper table. Government secrets and all. It made for dreadfully boring chit chat.

Cryptographer, Rory thought. *Grr! Pay the cop.* Cryptographer. *Part grey porch.* His mind scrambled and unscrambled the letters to form silly little anagrams. Anything to pass the time.

He wished time would pass a bit more quickly at the moment. It seemed as though he'd been sitting in the outer chamber of the rector's office forever. He nervously clicked the pen in his hand and stared at the rector's door. He hated being indoors! The fifteen-year old was a smashing athlete. He'd helped lead the Academy to a number of trophies. If it was an outdoor sport, Rory played. Unfortunately, he spent a bit more time on the field than in his textbooks. His marks were less than spectacular. So, now he was stuck here. Waiting. Inside. Sitting.

It wasn't that he didn't like books. On the contrary. He loved to read – stories about fantastic treasure hunts, grand adventure, or even mysteries. Anything that made him sneak a torch under his covers and read well into the wee hours of the morning. He wished he could venture off across the globe in search of treasure. Anything was better than being stuck here. He blew an errant strand of hair from his hazel eyes. The mere thought of spending even another thirty minutes indoors made his toes curl. He tossed the paper aside.

Something rustled across the room. Rory looked up. A pair of long crisply pressed black pant legs crossed beneath a newspaper Rory didn't recognize. He tried to decipher the foreign language, his forehead furrowing. He concentrated on one word in particular, framed against a black and white photograph of a fearsome-looking man.

Tesoro. Rory cocked one brown eyebrow. He struggled to recall his language lessons. Treasure?

Suddenly, a corner of the newspaper folded down.

"In a spot of trouble with the rector, are we?" the stranger spoke. It was the man from the photo!

Rory jumped. Staring down a crooked nose were the blackest eyes Rory had ever seen. As they pierced Rory's gaze, Rory shuddered perceptibly as if an Arctic draft breezed thru the room. But the thing that made Rory cringe was the livid white scar that ran from the tip of the stranger's eyebrow, hooking around his intense gaze, and crawled its way down the tanned canvas of his cheek like a fat pale snake. The stranger looked almost, well, sinister.

Rory gulped. Almost as if he could read Rory's mind, the man's face broke into a bright, white smile. He touched the scar with a leathery hand.

"Oh, don't mind this old thing. I caught the business end of a swordfish. Sport fishing in the Gulf of Mexico. I must confess. It was the 'one that got away'." The man chuckled.

Rory forced a grin, his eyes drifting back to the man's newspaper. The man's eyes followed Rory's gaze.

"Business interests in South America. I like to keep up with events." He flashed Rory another disarming grin. Rory grinned back. He supposed if you took away the deep-set eyes and frightening scar, the stranger looked like any other Edinburgh businessman in a three-piece suit.

Just then, the door to the rector's inner office opened.

Gordon Staid swung into the room, his great belly pressing forward like the prow of some great ocean-liner. Dunleavey chugged behind him like a dutiful tug. Staid quickly surveyed the room. His gaze fell on Rory. He impatiently waved his hand as if to dismiss an annoying insect.

"Oh, dear, Mr. Bruce, I'm afraid we will have to reschedule our appointment. It seems I have pressing business with Mr. Bluidy, here."

Rory barely took note of the rector's cursory introduction, cringing, rather, at the thought of having to return for another boring meeting. He rather do homework! He leapt to his feet.

"But, sir!" he protested.

"No. No. Back to class. Back to class!" Staid began to turn his back, when he suddenly grabbed the package from Dunleavey and pushed it into Rory's hands. "And be sure to deliver this. Straightaway."

He ushered Rory out toward the hallway, then turned his attentions back toward the mysterious stranger.

"Mr. Bluidy! How are you today, sir!" Staid blustered.

Rory craned his head back to see Bluidy set down his paper and stand, towering over the squat rector. What caught Rory's eye however, were the ebony walking stick Bluidy leaned on as he stood and the glint of the blood-red ruby eyes staring at him from the hollowed sockets of the polished silver skull at its top.

CHAPTER FIVE

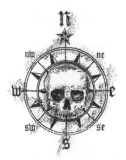

Bogey

The world population of nose pickers was divided into several different classes. There were the Sneakers. You know the ones. They peek to the left. They peek to the right. Then, when they are certain no one is looking, they dive in swiftly, pluck the offending crusty mucus from their nasal passages deposit it into a tissue and casually go about their business as if nothing has happened.

Then you had the Flickers. They were slightly less covert than the Sneakers when it came to the actual retrieval process, and even less so when it came to disposal. With the Flickers, the offensive matter was rolled between the fingers into a misshapen green ball of goo then flicked expertly, or not-so-expertly, across the room to a random target. Those less talented in the fine art of flicking quite often tagged a mass of curls hanging down the back of some unsuspecting girl.

But Sneakers and Flickers were amateurish aficionados when compared to the last group – the Miners. These were the serious pickers. They rolled up their sleeves, pointed an index finger straight up in the air with intent, and plunged in deep with no care for how they churned the weaker stomachs of those around them.

For Bogey McTavish, it was an art form. He even had his own sort of nasal mucus mural developing on the wall near his desk in the corner of the classroom. Only the especially juicy ones earned a position in the McTavish mural. His singular talent earned him his nickname – Bogey. His real name, of course, was Gavin, but only the teachers and his parents called him that. To everyone else, he was Bogey.

Of course, his peculiar hobby did not endear him to many of his classmates. Especially the girls. He had tried showing his masterpiece mural to Margaret Roy, the freckle-faced redhead in second-year Sciences, but she ran screaming toward the girls' bathroom. He had later heard on good authority that she spent two whole periods retching in the last stall. He didn't share his artwork anymore.

When he thought about it, Bogey wasn't even quite sure why he did it. He just knew it was far more exciting than History. Mr. Whitten droned on about some dreadfully boring royal. Bonnie Prince Charlie or something. Bogey chuckled. With a name like "Bonnie", Bogey supposed he was a bit of a nancy boy.

He flipped to the portrait in his history book. Stockings and curls.

Yep. A nancy boy, alright. Mr. Whitten mumbled something about the French sending money to help the Prince. Bogey raised an eyebrow.

Stockings, curls, and French? Bet he didn't get many dates with the ladies. The teacher mumbled along in a steady hum.

Bogey stifled a yawn. He propped a heavy head against his hand and surveyed the room, the day's lecture washing over him like a sedative. Through droopy eyes, he surveyed the classroom. Two rows over, Lenox Stuart had completely succumbed to Mr. Whitten's monotonous tone and now lay in a welling pool of drool. That was disgusting, Bogey thought.

In the front row, he noticed Patience Rayford slipping a folded note to her best chum, Annalise Mumford. No doubt it concerned the latest object of Patience's affection, some poor, unsuspecting chap who would soon be subjected to a week of fawning, love notes, and cutesy-wutsey girl gibberish. Girls took disgusting to a whole new level. Fortunately, a week was the approximate shelf-life of Patience's love-to-end-all loves. Bogey groaned. Patience was even more disgusting than Duncan's drool.

Suddenly, the hairs on the back of Bogey's

neck stood straight up on end. He swiveled his head. Maddagh Donaldson stared right at him. Bogey swallowed audibly, grateful for the barrier of three rows. Unfortunately, it was only a temporary reprieve, however. When the bell signaled first lunch, Bogey feared atomic wedgies, forfeiting his pocket change, or worse - swirlies in the loo.

Sweat began to bead on Bogey's forehead as Maddagh cracked the knuckles in his right fist. Each pop echoed with the finality of a guillotine drop. Bogey squirmed in his chair. Why was Maddagh even in this class? He looked like he was seventeen, if he was a day. Broad-chested with arms nearly the size of the One O'Clock gun atop Edinburgh Castle, there was no conceivable way Maddagh was only thirteen years old. Unless he was a genetic mutation, of course.

Bogey stifled a giggle as a grin tugged at the corners of his mouth. Maddagh certainly looked as if he could have been genetically spliced with an English bulldog. His cheeks hung in a slightly jowly fashion, and, come to think of it, he drooled a little when he spoke. Even his name, Maddagh, sounded a bit like "Mad Dog".

Bogey's giggle bubbled into a laugh. As he clapped his hand over his mouth, he swore Mad Dog growled. The even hum of Mr. Whitten's monotone stopped.

"Something amusing, Mr. McTavish?" the teacher asked.

Bogey bolted upright in his chair. He looked from his teacher to Mad Dog, who menacingly drew a finger across his neck, the universal sign for "you're going to get it".

Bogey looked quickly back to Mr. Whitten.

"Hiccups!" he squeaked. He cleared his throat and tried again. "Hic-hiccups, sir. May I get some - hic - water, please?" He looked toward Mad Dog, who wore the frustrated look of a hunter whose prey had just slipped the noose.

Mr. Whitten waved absent-mindedly. "Yes, yes. Of course. Be quick about it."

Bogey scrambled from his chair, skirted past Mad Dog, and scurried into the hall, Mad Dog leering all the way.

Once he had made it into the hall, Bogey sunk against the wall in relief and collected his thoughts. After a moment of slow, steadying breaths, Bogey straightened up, pointed his index finger straight up in the air, and started down the corridor.

CHAPTER SIX

Skeleton Key

He had searched everywhere, including some of the more revolting places - the boys' laundry room at the gymnasium - but the target of his hunt eluded him.

Rory heaved a sigh. He blew a bit of hair from his eye and leaned heavily against his locker. The first lunch bell pealed like a klaxon, and a sea of blue blazers erupted from classrooms and flooded the corridor.

"Some treasure hunter I'd make. I can't even

find one little boy. And he's probably right under my nose!"

Suddenly, his locker spoke. "Excuse me?"

Rory turned to the second year rifling through the locker next to him. "Did you say something?"

The boy shook his head and bustled off to his next class. Rory shook his head. He must be hearing things.

"I don't mean to be a bother, but I really have to use the loo."

Rory whipped impatiently toward the boy on his left. "If you have to go, than go!" he growled.

The boy backed away, brandishing his history text like a shield

"I'll go, if you say so, but some poor chap's cleats will be a bit soggy," the locker suggested.

Cleats, Rory thought. He had cleats in his locker. Oh, dear! He scrambled to open his locker door. He lifted the latch and yanked the door wide. An avalanche of books and athletic equipment tumbled out, all his.

A small boy, twisted like a Bavarian pretzel,

fell out awkwardly atop the heap.   Decidedly *not* his.

The boy adjusted his glasses and looked up at Rory.

"Thanks loads, chum," the pretzel spoke, untangling himself to an upright position.

"Yeah. Sure. No problem," Rory replied.

"The name's Colin. Colin McManus." Colin held out a hand in greeting. "But, most people call me Smout."

Rory shook his hand then abruptly rifled through the pocket of his blazer. He pulled out the mysterious package and presented it to Smout.

"This is for you," he stated rather matter-of-factly. As Smout took the package, Rory grinned and put his hands on his hips self-satisfied.   Maybe he wouldn't make such a bad treasure hunter after all.

Rector Staid hated pirates. Recent films had glorified them as dashing, debonair treasure hunters with ostentatious feather hats, lithe bodies, swarthy skin, and long, enviable locks. Staid ran a puffy hand over his thinning hair, and nudged his round little bowler hat to the side of his desk.

Not that Jack Bluidy resembled a certain rum-soaked, eccentric buccaneer captain, necessarily, but the livid scar across the man's face and his eerie, skull-topped cane, did lend particular credence to a pirate-like appearance.

Pirate, or no, all Staid knew was that one overcast day, a few weeks ago, a long limousine pulled up to the Academy and Bluidy presented the rector with a fat check to bolster the school's coffers. In the current economy, Staid was indifferent whether the money came from sound business investments or, indeed, from some rusty pirate's chest buried on a remote desert isle. An ironic grin settled at the corners of Staid's mouth as he acknowledged that one of the school's most famous alums, Robert Louis Stevenson, had gained notoriety writing perhaps the most famous pirate novel of all time.

Not to look a gift horse in the mouth, but Staid questioned Bluidy's motivation behind such a generous donation. Bluidy asserted that such a storied school with its pedigree of famous alums like

Sir Edward James Harland and R.M. Ballantyne deserved such a prize, but, indeed, the graduate that held the greatest fascination for Bluidy was, in fact, Stevenson.

After that initial visit, Bluidy continued to make odd appearances at the school, asking infinite questions about the author. What corners of the school did he like to frequent? Had any marks been found on school edifices that could be attributed to Stevenson? Staid, of course, had little information to offer on such remote historical topics, but he felt obligated to entertain Bluidy's impromptu visits.

Additionally, Bluidy frequently requested tours of the facilities, but his interest kept largely to those older sections of the school, like the main building of the Senior School. The odd request went further to unsettle the nervous rector, who now sat, staring uncomfortably, at the dapper businessman before him.

"So, Mr. Staid. I hope all goes well with my investment?" Bluidy tented his fingertips, touching them to his lower lip as his black eyes stared flatly at

Staid.

Staid swallowed to clear the lump lodged in his throat.

"Most certainly, Mr. Bluidy! We've managed to purchase new lab equipment for the Science Centre and stands for the Music School. Oh, and we had intended to fund a field expedition for our senior pupils out to the Scottish Seabird Centre - " Staid trailed.

"Had intended?" Bluidy leaned forward, his black eyes suddenly sparking feverishly.

Staid straightened.

"Yes. I'm afraid there's been a bit of a problem. A fly in the ointment, if you will."

Staid pulled uncomfortably at his tight collar. Bluidy did not look like a man who swatted at flies.

He looked like the sort that annihilated them.

Staid felt a sneeze tickling his nasal passages.

"I'm afraid there's been an incident on Fidra. Police business and all."

"I do hope it's nothing serious," Bluidy commented.

"Well, it appears someone has gone missing. The uncle of one of our students, I fear" Staid offered.

Bluidy settled back into the wingback, tenting his palms together in thought. "Well, now. That's interesting."

Smout ambled out of the boys' loo, checking that all things needing fastening were duly fastened. He scurried over to Rory, who leaned casually against a column.

"Thanks for offering to be my bodyguard to the lunchroom," Smout offered. He cracked his stiff neck from side to side. "Don't know that I could handle another stuffing today." They entered the crowded lunchroom, grabbed their trays and worked their way through the line. "Suppose it's a sight better than getting pantsed in front of the whole school, though."

The thought of standing in his knickers with his trousers pooled round his ankles made him shudder.

"No worries, chum. Mad Dog is a bit of a

nutter. Someone needs to put him back on his leash."

Smout nodded in hearty agreement as they weaved they way through.

"So, what happened, exactly?" Rory asked.

Smout shrugged. "Mad Dog stuffed me in the locker. Probably because I breathed in his direction. So, there I was, wedged in there like a kipper on his way to tea, and I heard the most peculiar sound. It sounded almost like," Smout paused.

"What? What did it sound like?" Rory urged, the curiosity bursting on his face.

"Well I can't be sure, but me mum used to always read *Treasure Island* to me."

Rory's eyes widened. "Are you serious? That's my favorite book!"

Smout smiled broadly. "Mine, too. Anyway, the sound I heard? Well, it was like what I always imagined Long John Silver's peg leg to sound like."

Rory blinked.

"Yeah, I know. I'm a bigger nutter than Mad Dog," he laughed. "Then everything went dark and I heard a voice. I was too scared silly to say anything."

"What did the voice say?" Rory asked.

"'It must be here. I must find it.' Then whoever it was walked away. Guess they didn't expect someone would be squashed in a locker listening."

"That sounds a bit dodgy."

Smout nodded in agreement. It certainly was a mystery, but it wasn't the only mystery facing the boys.

"So, what's in the package? Fancies from home?" Rory gestured to the twine-sealed parcel in Smout's pocket. Smout fished it out and examined the return address.

"Doubt it. It's from my uncle. More likely, it's a pygmy mask from Papua New Guinea, or a witch bottle from some blue-haired granny's backyard." Smout grabbed a red, shiny apple.

Rory shuddered as he reached for two milks. He handed one off to Smout. "A witch bottle? I hope it's not too cheeky, but what sort of chap is your uncle?"

"Oh, he's an archaeologist," Smout replied.

Rory exhaled in relief. "So was me mum."

"Was?" Rory questioned.

"I don't really talk about it much."

"Why?" Rory asked. "Is it positively awful?"

"No." Smout shrugged. "Just never really had anyone to talk to. She disappeared one night from the museum where she worked. Not a trace."

"That's right rank, mate," Rory exclaimed. "What about your dad?"

"Lost on a dig in South America. Least that's what Uncle Bernie tells me. I was so little when it happened."

"South America?" Rory pondered. "No, offense, Smout, but you've got rotten awful luck."

"Yeah," Smout agreed. "So, now, it's just Uncle Bernie and me. Two odd peas in pod. Bernie's all right though. Taught me how to sword fight."

"Cool."

"And I've learned loads from him. He even lets me help with his work sometimes," Smout continued. Rory grabbed a bit of dried jerky from the line, chewing absent-mindedly while Smout rambled. "Do you know he once got an entire crate of shrunken heads from the Jivaro Indian tribe in Ecuador?"

"Shrunken heads? Really? Like actual people heads?"

"They're called *tsantsa*. They're supposed to have magical powers. I always thought they just looked like beef jerky, though."

Rory stopped chewing.

"Someday I'll find me mum. The really awful bit, I suppose, is not knowing."

Rory opened his milk and raised it in a mock toast. "Well, here's to knowing the unknowable!" Smout grinned and started to open his milk as well. Rory grabbed his arm.

"No, wait. You have to open your package first!"

"Oh, yes!" Smout agreed. He yanked the twine from the bundle, stuffing it into his pocket then ripped the brown paper off in shreds. Under a wrapping of tissue, a large key thunked onto Smout's tray.

Rory raised a perplexed eyebrow as Smout picked up the strange key. It laid cold and heavy in his small hand. The brass shank of the key was long and pitted from age and exposure. The shank ended in a simple bit, flat and rectangular. But the part of the key that was most interesting to the two boys was the bow at the very top of the key. Rounded at the crest, thinning at the base, and grinning manically under hollowed eye sockets, was the symbol flown over scores of pirate ships over the centuries – a fearsome skull.

CHAPTER SEVEN

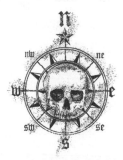

Cacklefruit and Bumboo

Emma Johnson sat at her usual table in the school dining hall, the second table in the second row. It was the golden mean of lunchroom seating. Meaning, of course, that the table sat squarely in the desirable middle between two extremes - the annoying and churlish boys and the twittering, frivolous girls. Quite frankly, both groups gave Emma a rather acidic stomach.

She presumed the plump, young girl a few seats over, the sole remaining occupant of the table, shared her opinion. Emma attempted an awkward smile, and watched as the girl opened her peanut butter sandwich and unloaded an entire packet of sugar onto it. Emma cleared her throat.

"Did you know that the average person consumes nearly 35 kilograms of sugar per year? I'm quite certain it's one of the contributing factors to the ongoing obesity problems in most middle-income populations," Emma offered generously.

The girl shot her a withering stare and shuffled to the far end of the table. She munched down quite purposefully on her calorie-laden sandwich and smacked loudly with an open mouth in Emma's direction.

"Well! There's no need to be rude!" Emma huffed and turned her attentions back to her well-balanced and nutritious lunch of vegetable curry, Greek yoghurt, a boiled egg, and a variety of fresh fruits. Peanut butter and sugar, indeed!

She fished a book from her satchel. Books made far better companions than people. They didn't giggle over silly boys. They didn't act like total prats over silly games. And they didn't intentionally digest foolish amounts of tooth-rotting sugar.

Emma stole a glance at Peanut Butter Girl. She was rewarded with an open mouthful of masticated peanut butter and bread. Yes, books were far better companions.

She sighed. Of course, there was one person with whom she might like to interact. Her gaze travelled toward the lunch line where a tall boy stood next to a smaller, spindly one. Rory Bruce was different. Emma was certain. Yes, he was an athlete, but Emma frequently saw him with his nose buried in a book, a definite plus. And he was being so nice to that younger chap. Emma wondered what the two were discussing so intently. The younger boy held something in his hands, but Emma couldn't quite make out what. She actually stared rather fixedly when Rory cast a glance in her direction. He smiled and Emma flushed, immediately lowering her gaze. Okay, maybe she wasn't quite ready to interact. She decided to stick to her books.

Emma shook herself from her reverie, and

propped open the history book she'd been reading. In Emma's opinion, which she regarded with some merit, knowing your past was very important. You couldn't very well expect to know where you were going without knowing where you had already been. As any moderately intelligent person would realize, you would only end up going in circles, like a dog chasing its tail.

The book's topic centered on 16th century pirates who terrorized the Scottish coasts. Though she was unlikely to admit it to anyone else, Emma really liked pirates. Well, the adventure of them anyway. They were so much braver than she could ever hope to be. The idea of actually risking life and limb for ill-gotten riches made her erupt in berry-red hives. She supposed that's why she loved her books so much. They were safe. Let others take the risks, like the gentlemen of fortune who had sailed with Bartholomew Roberts, the infamous "Black Bart." Those scalawags sailed into Scottish waters, but were captured by those loyal to the Crown. Tossed into the dank dungeons of Edinburgh Castle, most met their end at the swinging end of a hangman's noose, their fortunes taking a turn for the worse. Emma shuddered involuntarily at the image of necks snapped at the gallows when, suddenly, a beefy hand clapped down on her shoulder.

"Caw! That's nasty!" a deep, guttural voice declared behind her. Dreading the answer, Emma turned to identify the speaker.

"Maddagh Donaldson. I might have suspected. Don't worry. It's nothing you'd be interested in. It's called a book." Emma scoffed.

The intended insult fell on deaf ears. Mad Dog's group of cronies, each with a stare more vacant than the next, chortled gleefully as Mad Dog snatched the pirate book from the table. He turned it this way and that, looking at the pictures of overflowing treasure chests and the triumphant grins of pirate kings surrounded by beautiful women.

"Oh, I don't know. Seems like I could like this quite a bit, this pirate business. That's something a guy like me could look forward to, you know?" Mad Dog asserted. He continued to hold it just out of

Emma's reach. She hopped up and down like a hungry bird after a worm.

"Look forward to?" Emma snorted. "A life of scurvy and rickets, maggot-infested hardtack, never having a place to truly call home, all to be clapped in irons and meet your end swinging like a pendulum at the bottom of the hangman's noose?"

Mad Dog blinked. His chums stared blankly. Then Mad Dog broke the silence.

"For a chance at all that gold? That'd be absolutely spiffing!" Mad Dog crowed. The group of boys guffawed. One slapped Mad Dog on the back. Emma narrowed her gaze at the unruly boys.

"You are an absolute git, Maddagh Donaldson. No wonder they call you Mad Dog."

A sudden hush fell over the boys. Several took a wary step back. Mad Dog purpled, his jowls puffing in building anger.

"Nobody...calls me... Mad Dog," he growled. Emma lowered a stare at him and grinned mischievously. She positively couldn't resist.

"Woof."

The next few moments seemed to pass in slow motion.   Mad Dog's mouth stretched in a Spartan battle cry. From across the room, Smout and Rory looked up from their strange discovery. Rory grabbed Smout's arm.

"Stay here," he urged. Smout nodded, watching as Rory sprinted across the room toward Emma and Mad Dog. Smout panicked. Rory had taken off with the key.

"Rory! Wait!" he cried and scrambled after him.

Back at the table, Mad Dog lobbed Emma's book into the air. Emma lunged for it. Mad Dog lunged for Emma. The book arced over Emma's head making a sure line for the Greek yoghurt. Emma twisted, yanking the tray from certain disaster. The boiled egg sprang from its roost, twirling end over end, and landed on the floor directly under the foot of one of Mad Dog's compatriots. The boy lost purchase, his arms flailing. He landed hard on the table behind him, startling the third years sitting there and turning their table into a juice-loaded catapult.

At that moment, Rory stretched out horizontally, making a graceful dive for Emma's book. It landed with a soft thud in his arms. Emma sighed gratefully, but her relief was short-lived. A waterfall of sailing grape juice cascaded onto Rory's head, turning Emma's book a lovely shade of splotched lavender.

Then time froze.

Time froze, that is, until the banshee wail screeching from Emma's throat sent students diving for cover, hands clasped protectively over their ears. She grabbed the Greek yoghurt and hurled it at Mad Dog, who ducked it with an agility quite impressive for his size. The yoghurt missed its intended target. Instead, it splattered all over Smout, turning his glasses into yoghurt-smeared blinders. He floundered about, knocking into someone's macaroni casserole. A hundred cheesy projectiles peppered the air, landing on a variety of surprised students. The air filled with alternating squeals and cheers.

Bogey strolled into the lunch room at that very moment. An airborne noodle landed on his blue blazer, sliding downward in a cheesy, yellow trail.

He plucked the noodle from the jacket and popped it into his mouth.

"Mmm. Fast food," he declared and chewed with gusto before joining the melee.

CHAPTER EIGHT

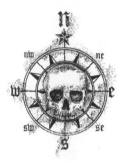

Scallywags

The day was turning into an unmitigated disaster. A visit from Bluidy, a cancelled field expedition, now a food fight? Gordon Staid's perfectly ordered Academy was disintegrating fast. And he was completely out of tissues!

He gave half a thought to wiping his nose with one of the infinite papers Dunleavey shoved before him for signature. The rector admitted, he didn't know the man too well. The odd looking chap just recently joined the school staff. Come to think of it, it had been just after Bluidy first appeared at the school.

The rector was distracted from the thought by the Adam's apple bobbling on Dunleavey's ridiculously thin neck. The secretary's beaky nose protruded from a long, horsey face. As Dunleavey set each successive paper in front of him, the repetitive bobbing reminded Staid of one of those drinking bird toys. The ones that perpetually rocked up and down to nip a bit of water.

Staid rubbed his watery eyes to dispel the bizarre image. His nose pulsated, red enough to signal ships on the coast. He might have to consider a visit to his allergist if things kept on this way, he thought.

The allergy-burdened rector took a moment to survey the motley group gathered in his office. The five students sat in five identical chairs lined up facing his desk. Some faces presented with familiarity. Others made their debuts.

Maddagh Donaldson, of course, was a frequent flyer. The son of a locksmith, Maddagh often found himself on the wrong side of the rules. He used lock picking skills learned from his father to access all sorts of trouble. Exploding bubbly bangs in the faculty lounge. Turning the milk in the cafeteria into glue. Who knew there were so many creative applications for vinegar?

The rector shook his head. A shame, really, he thought. For such a delinquent, Maddagh had a fine mind for scientific principles. If only he'd apply himself properly.

Of course, there was Rory Bruce. The hero. The rector squirmed. The athlete reminded the portly headmaster of less appetizing days as a chubby lad, lagging behind fitter children during Athletics. Mr. Bruce argued he had simply rushed to the rescue of Miss Johnson, a quiet, normally solitary pupil. Staid couldn't determine if that was by design, or if she was simply incapable of meeting another's eye. Currently, she stared quite fixedly at the ornate pattern on the Oriental rug, refusing to look at anyone else.

Gordon McTavish, a second year, seemed to

be particularly enthralled with something up his nose at the moment. The rector found himself wishing fervently he had not run out of tissues. Though Mr. McTavish had been involved in the food fiasco only peripherally, Staid had brought him in on principal.

Then there was Colin McManus. Smout, the rector had heard some of the student's call him. The young man blinked at him from behind a pair of the most enormous yoghurt-crusted glasses the rector had ever seen. He was a scrawny little whelp, and in light of the circumstances, he couldn't help but feel a bit of pity for him.

But small or no, there was no excuse for disorder.

"Your collective behavior is absolutely intolerable!" Staid bellowed. "What do you have to say for yourselves?"

Emma opened her mouth to speak, but the blustering little man cut her off.

"This is an absolute disgrace! I have half a mind to expel the lot of you!" The proclamation elicited a variety of reactions from the group.

Emma cringed.

Mad Dog grinned.

Rory grimaced.

Smout nervously fingered the heavy key in his pocket.

Bogey nailed a gold leaf statue across the room with a well-aimed flick. The rector shuddered.

"Instead, since this entire incident seems to have stemmed from an inability to get along with our fellow man, I have devised, I believe, a rather clever solution. You five scalawags will participate in a collective service project. Perhaps spending some time together will help you overcome your differences and exercise something I like to call tolerance!"

Mad Dog leapt to his feet, voice rising in protest. "You're barking mad! Spend time with this sorry lot? I'm not working with these gits!"

Emma and Rory joined in the objection wholeheartedly. Staid just sat back into his chair, smiling broadly.

"There. You see? It's begun working

already. You are already agreeing on something. It settled then. The project starts tomorrow. Mr. Dunleavey here will be your chaperone."

Dunleavey stood straight up, eyes wide. Apparently, babysitting was not in his job description.

"B-b-but, sir!" he babbled. "I hardly think I'm qualified."

"Codswallop, Dunleavey," Staid responded. He turned back to the children.

"Report bright and early in this office, straightaway after roll call. You will receive your marching orders then. As for the rest of today, consider yourselves suspended."

Emma looked as though the rector had passed a death sentence. She would have preferred walking the plank.

"Now, all of you remain here, while I notify your parents of your shenanigans," Staid grumbled. "Colin, I'm afraid I need you to come with me for a moment."

He wrapped an arm around Smout's shoulders and guided him into the outer office.

Once the rector had cleared the room, Dunleavey stumbling behind him, Emma twisted in her chair to face Mad Dog.

"This is all your fault. If you weren't such a cretin," she began.

"Hah!" Mad Dog burst. "Shows what you know, smarty-pants. I'm not even from Yugoslavia!"

"That's cretin, not Croatian, you dolt!" Emma shook her head as Smout shuffled back into the room. Rory rushed to his side.

"What's going on?"

Smout's eyes welled with tears behind his smudged glasses. "It's my uncle. He's gone missing. The rector says they're sending the police round to fetch me back to the flat."

Rory whistled low. "I take it back. Your luck's not just rotten. I think you're positively cursed. Maybe it was the *tsantsa*."

The children fell silent. Smout pulled the skeleton key from his pocket. As he did, the length of twine, with its odd little knot, fell to the floor. Emma reached down to retrieve it.

"What's that you've got there? A chocolate bar?" Mad Dog sidled over toward Smout. "I could fancy a bit of nosh about now. All that food flying about, and not a bit went in my belly."

"Mind your mitts, mate," Rory warned. "And show a bit of sympathy, right?"

"It's a key," Bogey offered. "And a right strange one, at that."

"Well," Mad Dog asked. "What's it open?"

"I don't really know," Smout answered. "My Uncle Bernie sent it to me wrapped in a package. No note. Just the key. And now, he's missing."

"Wonky," Bogey theorized. "Looks the type to open a treasure chest or something."

A funny little hush fell over the group.

Rory cocked his head. "Now, that's a bit odd."

"What's odd?" Smout asked.

"Well," Rory began as he ruffled his hair in puzzlement. "When I was in the rector's office yesterday, there was a man here. A bit scary looking, if you ask me. Had a twisty scar on his face.

Anyway, he was reading a foreign paper, Spanish I think. I couldn't make out much, but I did catch one word...treasure. Don't know who he was, but he sure had the rector's knickers in a twist."

The group pondered Rory's information for a few moments.

"The package," Emma suddenly spoke. "Was it wrapped in this string?"

She held up the twine.

Smout nodded. "Yeah. That was wrapped around the package."

Emma's eyes grew wide. "Do you know what this is? This knot?"

The boys shook their heads collectively. Emma rushed toward them.

"It's called a monkey's fist. See how it looks like a paw?"

Bogey sniggered. "A paw? Well you'll know all about that, won't you, Mad Dog?"

His comment was rewarded with a slap to the back of the head.

Emma continued. "This kind of knot, it's

used as a weight for a heaving line. You know. On ships?"

She groaned as she waited for the neurons to fire across synapses. Boys could be so slow.

"Like pirate ships?" she offered.

The boys jumped as though electrocuted.

"Pirates?" they mouthed together.

Emma nodded vehemently. "Yes! They formed the knot around a weight, like a rock, or a small piece of paper. Maybe your uncle sent you a message after all!"

She handed the rope to Smout.

"Well, go ahead. Open it," Rory poked Smout.

Five heads lowered over the strange little knot. Smout's thin fingers worked at the intricate weaves. The children gasped in unison as a tightly folded wad of yellowed paper tumbled into Smout's open hand.

He carefully opened the paper and flattened it.

"It's a bit of map," Mad Dog said. Two mermaids danced on waves holding a framed scale of nautical miles. A wreck of seabirds floated on the water beneath the scale, wings poised for flight. Several fishes, their mouths yawning, bobbled through the waves. The most tantalizing feature of the scrap, however, was the rounded tip of land, just a teasing portion, peering out from the lower edge of the map.

"Well that's not a lot of information to go on," Rory stated.

"And it doesn't say anything about the key," Bogey sighed.

"I'll say this much. If you blokes have a mind to go treasure hunting, I'm all in," Mad Dog stated rather matter-of-factly.

"Are you mad?" Rory blustered. "Who said anything about treasure hunting?" But the fever burning in his eyes gave away his excitement. Mad Dog smiled conspiratorially. Rory huffed.

"Anyway, what makes you think we'd include a nutter like you in on anything?"

"Well, the way I see it is this. Either you include me in, or this 'nutter' squeals to the rector."

Mad Dog folded his arms self-satisfactorily. A few interminable moments passed as the children eyeballed one another, then the scrap of map.

"Doesn't look like we have much choice, then," Rory said. The other nodded in agreement.

"Wait! Look!" Smout cried. "Here! On the back. There's something written." He held it up to the light.

"What does it say?" Emma asked.

Smout's squinted, trying to read past the yoghurt smudges on his glasses. He smeared them on the edge of his blue blazer, trying to clear them. A puzzled look passed over his face as he read the words out loud.

"Only Blind Pew can read Billy's Bones."

CHAPTER NINE

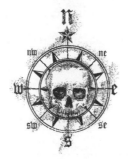

Dead Man's Chest

He watched them, the group of five, as they left the Academy. He watched them from behind the dark, tinted windows. The small boy, the one they called Smout, shifted nervously from one foot to the other as he waited. McManus had sent something to the boy. He was certain of it. But what?

One by one, the children departed, escorted by shouting, finger-wagging parents. All except Smout.

When the police car pulled up to the curb with its rotating gumball of blue light, the watcher shifted in his seat. The school's rector held the boy on the curb until the constable stepped out and led him to the back seat. The official exchanged a few words with the rector, shook hands, and returned to his car, driving off toward the city centre. The rector remained on the curb, watching the vehicle drive away, then suddenly erupted in another violent sneeze.

The long, black limousine that had been parked across the street, pulled away, heading in the same direction as the police car and the small boy with the secret.

It was like being squashed between two great, powder-scented pillows. Miss Dumbarton had crushed Smout in a smothering, motherly hug the moment the constable had deposited him on the front stoop.

Smout turned a mooshed face toward the policeman, and mouthed the words, "Help me!". The young officer, shook his head, having just taken a wary step backward, fearing he might be enveloped into a similar, eau-de-lilac vise.

"Oh, Smout! Smout, Smout, Smout! Dearest boy! Thank the stars you're alright!" Miss Dumbarton prattled. Smout gained a momentary reprieve as she suddenly held him at arms length, assessing any potential damage. She looked him up and down, and apparently satisfied with the results, reached to embrace him once more. Smout was quicker this time, ducking just out of reach. Miss Dumbarton clucked her tongue and patted the apron across her wide mid-section.

"Yes, well, now. Such awful news about your Uncle Bernie. And after that nasty business with your mum. Just up and vanished!" She threw her hands into the air in punctuation. "What's the world coming to? Well, don't you worry now, love. I'm sure he'll turn up, right as rain!" She patted Smout's head. "Thank you, Constable, for bringing him home safe. Care for a spot of tea? Perhaps some cheese? I'm sure I can rustle up a wedge from somewhere." Her voice trailed as she looked toward the interior of the flat.

The policeman looked at Smout for advice.

Smout shook his head forcefully.

"Thank you, Mum, but no. Got to get back to the case and whatnot," the young man told her. He turned to Smout, placing a hand on his shoulder. "Good luck, mate."

Smout nodded his thanks, but secretly thought as he patted his pocket, who needs luck when you have a map?

"Ouch!" Rory exclaimed as Bogey bent his ear down with a sneaker.

"Sorry 'bout that," Bogey offered as he steadied himself on a discarded stack of crates and boxes. "Was trying to sneak a better look. Crikey, that's a lot of coppers."

The two boys hid behind a dustbin in the nearby alley. They watched as police trailed in and out of the flat, looking like busy ants on a hill. They saw Smout get squashed by a large, blue-haired woman, then pat his pocket.

Rory shoved Bogey. "There! That's the signal! Come on!"

Bogey teetered on his perch then tumbled like dominoes. The resulting crash echoed off the brick walls. The boys dove behind the dustbin as a couple of the police looked in their direction, one very tall in a MacIntosh, the other shorter, scribbling furiously on a notepad.

"What's that?" Scribbles asked.

"Dunno. Go have a look" ordered MacIntosh.

"Why me?" Scribbles whined.

"Because I outrank you. Now, go have a look!"

Back in the alley, Rory thumped Bogey upside the head. "Some spy you are."

The two boys froze as Scribbles strolled their way. Rory pressed back against the wall, melding with the brick. Scribbles almost peered round the corner of the dustbin, when MacIntosh waved him back.

Scribbles abandoned his search and shrugged.

"Bloomin' cats, no doubt," he muttered.

As Scribbles retuned to his partner's side, MacIntosh jabbed his thumb towards the inside of the flat.

"Smith's just told me they've searched, but found nothing of interest to the case. There's an odd chest of some sort, but it's locked. Housekeeper says it's full of old research papers and the like. Says the key's been lost for years. Probably nothing. I say let's go. We're done here."

Scribbles nodded and the policemen moved off. Rory smacked Bogey in the chest.

"Did you hear that? A locked chest? With no key? Come on! We've got to get in there!"

"What about the others?" Bogey asked, his eyes searching.

At that moment, Emma raced up behind them. "Here I am. Mad Dog's trailing behind. The git."

Mad Dog sauntered up to the gathered group. "I'm just taking my time. It's part of my plan. Let you blokes do all the work, then I collect the loot. Wouldn't want to over-tax myself, you know."

"Then you might not want to use one's entire vocabulary in one sentence then," Emma quipped. The other boys laughed as Mad Dog grumbled.

"Alright, come on. He's given the signal." Rory waved them forward.

The signal had been arranged after they discovered the mysterious clue hidden inside the monkey's fist. They had agreed to meet secretly at Smout's flat.

"If my uncle sent this to me, he did it for a reason. I mean to find out what," Smout declared. The others pledged to help him on his quest.

They snuck along the wall, headed for the back of Smout's building. They reached the back door through a small, disheveled garden of lavender and thistledown. Miss Dumbarton wasn't a very good gardener either. Rory gave three sharp raps on the door and waited for it to open.

An eternity passed before the door creaked horror-movie wide. The resolve of the assembled group wavered ever so slightly, half-expecting a hunchbacked ogre to materialize from the dark interior. Instead, Smout poked his cow-licked head outside. The children breathed a collective sigh of relief.

"It's about time!" Mad Dog fussed as Smout
ushered them inside the dark interior of the flat.

"Give it a rest, Maddagh!" Smout whispered
tersely. "I had to wait till the police left. They've
been all over the flat. Mind the mud."

He led them through the anteroom, a pair of
Uncle Bernie's mud-covered wellies standing
patiently in the corner as if waiting for their owner to
step into them and trek into the Scottish countryside.

"Did anyone have any trouble getting away?"
Smout whispered. Everyone shook their heads.

"I want you to know, I really appreciate this,"
Smout continued.

"Wasn't like I had other plans for the
afternoon," Mad Dog grinned remorsefully. "'Cept
getting yelled at by me dad. So, I turned up the
stereo, snot-shakin' loud and climbed out my
bedroom window. He's probably yelled himself
purple through the door by now."

Emma sighed. "Mother is somewhere in the
Grassmarket working her way through the shops. Her
reprimand began somewhere in between the decision

over red or black cashmere. It dwindled somewhere during the great debate over open-toed heels or the classic pump. I told her if I couldn't be in school, I was off to the library to study. Don't think I had her attention as much as the handbag she was fondling when I left," Emma sighed.

Bogey sniggered, earning him a withering look from Emma. He cringed.

"Mum was fairly chuffed. Dad's out of town on mission," Rory volunteered.

"Mission?" Mad Dog laughed. "What is he? Some sort of spy?"

"Yeah. That's right. A codebreaker's what he is."

"You're a cheeky liar! No way your dad's as cool as that. I mean, look at you."

Rory made to lunge for Mad Dog, but Emma placed a gentle hand on his arm.

"It's okay, Rory," she began. "I believe you."

Everyone looked at Bogey, who just shrugged. "Gran just watches the telly all day. Unless I'm a bon-bon, not likely she'll even notice."

They passed through a narrow hallway papered in a wild floral. Cock-eyed photos of Smout as a baby hung hodgepodge on the wall. In many of them, he was bookended by two smiling adults, a large, strapping man with dark hair and a petite, fair-haired woman with bright eyes.

"Is that your mum and dad?" Bogey asked, pointing to a photo of Smout and his family on a beach. Smout's parents beamed broadly as an infant Smout waved a sand shovel in the air with one hand and a tightly sealed clam in the other.

Smout nodded. "Yeah. I suppose I was born to dig for treasure."

The group rounded the corner into the living room. Emma gasped.

They surveyed the over-turned sofa cushions, the scrabble of crumpled papers littered about the waste can and the trail of books strewn about the room.

Mad Dog snickered. "Whoa. The cops really tossed the place, didn't they?" Emma wrinkled her nose in disgust at a crust of sandwich that had most certainly fossilized.

Smout shrugged. "Naw. It's always like this."

Emma threw her hands up in despair. "How are we supposed to find any clues in this rubble? We don't even know exactly what we're looking for."

"That's not entirely true," Rory began. "We heard a couple of the bobbies outside mention something about a locked chest. Your uncle have anything like that?"

Smout's eyes widened as he shook his head. "Yeah, he does. Follow me."

He took them down to the basement, down a cold, dank stairway. Smout shuddered then coughed, taking a draught on his inhaler. "I hardly ever come down here. Uncle Bernie says it's not safe."

Mad Dog elbowed his way to the front of the group. "Well, I'm all in then. Let's get cracking. Whoa!"

The large boy stopped. There, in a cobwebbed corner of the dark room, sat an old, leather chest, bound in pockmarked brass. At the center of the chest, yawning blackly, was a keyhole. A keyhole just large enough to fit the key Smout held in his hand.

CHAPTER TEN

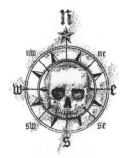

Bilge Rat

The trail led deep into the cavernous recesses of the castle. It was thin, much like the rat that had made it. In fact, it was a quest for food that had led the rat into this deep part of the castle, past the stone walls that began here, at the base of the castle, and climbed through the dark, dolerite stone of the long extinct volcano.

The rat rose on his haunches, whiskers twitching at some alien smell then scurried along the rough hewn wall.

Rats were no stranger to Edinburgh. In fact, many years ago, teeming numbers of black rats were harbingers of doom for the city as the fleas they carried spread a terrible sickness called the plague. Ghosts of plague victims were rumored to haunt certain areas of the city now. Unexplained noises and lights, and things that went bump in the night had even earned Edinburgh its title as "most haunted city in Europe."

A low, eerie moan echoed through the murky, stone passageways. The rat froze. A wavering light flickered on the wall, shadows dancing a macabre waltz. The rat shot off into the dark, abandoning his search for food.

As the light grew brighter, the shadows on the wall grew enormous. They were misshapen and distorted, an underworld nightmare. The light shuddered as wraithlike tendrils of black twisted their way through a set of iron bars set into the stone, an ancient prison cell.

Inside the cell, a vague lump huddled in the far corner. As the grasping fingers of the shadow reached it, a raspy groan rose from the crouched figure.

"Go ahead. Moan." A strangely accented voice echoed from another corner of the dungeon. "No one will hear you. You are in the belly of the castle."

A short, brown arm hung a lantern on a hook embedded on the wall. The arm was connected to a short, lumpy man. His squat frame resembled a dollop of dough plopped on the spot, pulled out of shape by gravity. One eye drooped lazily, giving him a permanent half-asleep look. He wore a stained lab coat, smudged with oil and grease, the perfect picture of a mad scientist.

The shadowy lump inside the cell groaned and lifted a disheveled head. "You'll never find the gold."

His captor giggled maniacally. "Oh, but you see, Mr. McManus, that is where you and I disagree."

The man in the lab coat waddled away. He approached a steel table where an odd, wheeled box sat gleaming mysteriously in the lantern light. He patted the top of the odd contraption, his gaze running the length of the device. At the end of a long, jointed arm, a menacing hook waited, poised for action.

"My benefactor has invested quite a tidy sum of money in my work because he believes we will find the gold. With or without your assistance, Mr. McManus. And my little *Piratino* here will be the one to do it"

"You're mad," McManus laughed. "Mad as a hatter. Even if the technology did exist, you need the clues to even know where to look."

"I am not mad! You are merely too much of a simpleton to understand how my clever device works. You will see. I will find the treasure. Then perhaps then people will stop laughing at me." He stroked the robotic device lovingly, like a child.

"And if someone else beats you to the treasure?" McManus pressed.

The man in the lab coat smiled, a crooked eyebrow raising over his lazy eye. He tapped several strokes on the nearby keyboard.

"Well, then, *Piratino* will take care of them,

too."

The robot's sharp hook snapped menacingly.

CHAPTER ELEVEN

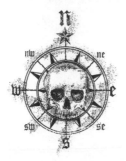

Billy's Bones

"Well? Are you going to open it, or what?" Mad Dog burst. The silence that had fallen over the group exploded into a cacophony of voices as everyone began urging Smout to use the key and unlock the mysterious chest. He shrugged them off, waving him arms wildly.

"Alright! Alright! Get off!" he bellowed. "We have no idea what's in that chest."

"Well, you won't know what's in it until you open it, now will, you?" Mad Dog offered. "And people say I'm the slow one."

Emma grimaced. "Oh, go ahead and open it, Smout. What's the worst that could happen?"

Everyone glowered at her.

"Alright then. Let's have a peek." Smout wiped his hands on his trousers and fished the key from his pocket.

Everyone held their breath as Smout slid the odd key into the waiting lock. He gave it a smart turn and the latch snicked open. Smout placed two sweaty palms on the edge of the large chest lid, sucked in a wheezy breath, and pushed the lid open.

Jumbled inside was an odd assortment of yellowed papers, well-thumbed notebooks, a hodge-podge of notes and musings on items of historical significance. The bric-a-brac one would expect to find among the belongings of an archaeological scholar. The children each grabbed a stack of the dusty papers, searching for something, anything, that would shed light on their quest.

Mad Dog eventually stood, tossing a ream to the ground in disgust. "Aw, there's nothing here! Just a bunch of boring gibberish. Where's the treasure, Smout?"

Emma was engrossed in a paper on Mary Queen of Scots. "Mad Dog, this is treasure. After a fashion. There are some really neat ideas on scads of archaeological mysteries," she offered.

Mad Dog snatched the paper from her hands. "Let me see that!"

"Emma's right," Rory agreed. "Look. There's research here on the lost city of Atlantis, the Oak Island money pit, even the treasure of the Knights Templar! If someone were to find all this, they'd be richer than the Queen!"

Smout shrugged. "Uncle Bernie loved mysteries. Seems like everyone in my family did. It was like a game."

"Games, huh?" Bogey piped from the bottom of the chest, his top half hidden below the lip of the chest. His legs kicked awkwardly as he lost his balance and toppled through the open lid. "Oof!"

His head popped out of the chest. Held in his hand was a small canvas bag. "Any of them fancy dominoes?"

"What?" Smout asked. The children gathered around as Smout took the bag from Bogey. He shook the contents into his hand, six worn ivory dominoes.

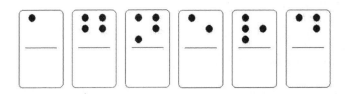

"Only six?" Mad Dog groused. "Rubbish. Not even a full set. Couldn't even lay out a decent boneyard with six."

Rory grabbed Mad Dog's arm. "What? What's that you just said?"

Mad Dog slowly removed his arm from Rory's grip, eyes narrowed.

"I said," Mad Dog began slowly, "that six isn't even enough to lay out a decent boneyard, but if you don't keep your mitts off my arm, I'm sure we could find a few more bones to add."

Rory gulped. Emma whacked Mad Dog with a rolled newspaper.

"Behave, boys." She took one of the dominoes from Smout's outstretched hand. "Hang on. This is strange. Some of the pips have been scratched off. See here. The black dots have been picked clean away. You suppose it means something?"

She handed the tile back to Smout who laid the dominoes out in a neat line on the floor. He pushed them around, forming a number of combinations with the random dots. The answer skirted around the edges of Smout's mind, just out of reach. He closed his eyes, trying to pull a pattern from the blind darkness.

Suddenly, his eyes popped wide open. "Blind Pew!"

The sudden outburst startled his companions, and everyone tumbled backward. The white, ivory tiles scattered in different directions. Smout scrambled to gather them back together.

"Blind Pew? The rat what gave Billy Bones the black spot in that pirate story?" Mad Dog questioned. Smout nodded.

"Exactly! 'Only Blind Pew can read Billy's Bones.' Don't you see? Or, rather, don't see? It's Braille, and the dominoes are the bones! Uncle Bernie changed them up to leave another clue."

"Of course!" Emma agreed. "I did a report on Louis Braille last term. I know all the letters."

"Well, what does it say?" Bogey pushed.

"A-G-N-E-R-D," Emma spelled.

Smout looked at the regiment of dominoes.

"Well, I doubt that's it. What about R-E-D-N-A-G?" Mad Dog offered.

"Red nag?" Bogey questioned. "Why do you suppose his uncle would leave a message about a red horse, you twit?"

"It was just a guess," Mad Dog stated.

Smout brain raced. He knew Uncle Bernie had left him a message in the dominoes, but what?

"Rory, you said your dad's into codes. Can you make any sense of this?" Smout asked the older boy.

"Dunno. Let me have a go at it," Rory replied. He shuffled the dominoes, grouping and regrouping the letters like one of his anagrams. He suddenly paused and pointed to the last arrangement "Um, Smout? Have a look at this."

The color drained from Smout's face. The proper order of the letters became crystal clear.

D-A-N-G-E-R.

CHAPTER TWELVE

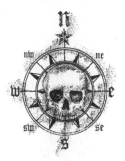

Gold Fever

No one appreciated a good book anymore, Fergus Ofxam thought as he surveyed the vacant interior of his little bookshop. Children these days were more enthralled with the beeps and blips of their video games, computer-generated effects, and Saturday morning cartoons. He stared out the plate glass window as large, wet raindrops smacked fatly against the gilt words lettered there. *Gubbins Corner: Rare Books and Collectibles*.

Rare, indeed. On the sporadic occasion

someone did venture into the shop tucked neatly in a corner off Edinburgh's Royal Mile, they often erroneously addressed him as Mr. Gubbins. It wasn't his name, of course. They merely assumed that the store window bore the name of its owner. He seldom exerted the energy to correct them. He simply rang up their sale, deposited their books into a sack, and sent them back out into the bustling thoroughfare.

In fact, the store garnered its name from the eclectic assortment of dusty titles that inhabited its shelves. There were travel books, books on history, adventure titles, romance novels, children's picture books, new books that still smacked of the glue binding their pages, and first editions whose hand-stitching had yellowed through the years – a vast assortment of odds and ends – a gubbins.

Fergus himself was a hodgepodge assortment of pieces parts. His round head resembled an over-inflated balloon, too large atop his small shoulders. Wispy tufts of white hair erupted here and there in patches, though it appeared that more insistent hair grew from his nose and ears. A pince-nez, which he had the nervous habit of polishing with the edge of his patched sweater vest, balanced on the tip of his beaked nose. A paunch, well-padded by seventy-odd years of fattening cakes and sweets, lipped over his belt. It hardly seemed possible that his thin legs could support a feather, let alone the weight of the odd, little store owner.

But, support him they did as the old man tottered with his steaming tea cup to the overstuffed armchair nestled next to the hearth. An orange tabby cat swirled between his legs, searching for attention. Mr. Oxfam set the tea down and eased himself into the chair, reaching for the mewling feline. The locket hanging from the cat's collar gave a cheery jingle as Fergus pulled the ball of fur onto his lap.

"Ah, Flint. How are you today, old friend? Catch any mice?" Fergus mumbled affectionately. He fingered a well-placed scratch behind the cat's ear, judging from the contented purr that rumbled from the tabby's throat. Leaning forward, Fergus grabbed the poker and gently stoked the glowing embers in the fireplace. A brilliant, golden-red flame erupted.

"Ah, now that's better." The old man purred himself, and settled back into the plump cushions. He picked up the old book resting on the side table, opened it to a marked page, and began reading.

"Fifteen men on a dead man's chest. Yo, ho, ho, and a bottle of rum."

The few inches of rum left in the bottle sloshed in amber waves before settling placidly to the bottom. The light from the bulkhead lamp filtered through his glass, casting golden shimmers on the polished wooden table before him. He tried to trap the jewel-like reflections with a finger, but they ghosted out of reach with each roll of the waves under the boat. Then they glimmered back into existence, taunting him. Teasing him. Showing him that which he so desperately desired then hiding it from him again. Gold.

Jack Bluidy had gold fever.

Most people didn't bother hunting for treasure. The risk was too daunting. The odds too long. The obsession either pulsed within your veins, or you suddenly woke up one day and realized your true calling. As for Jack Bluidy, he was driven by both. The passion for treasure burned deep within, and nothing could stand in his way.

He'd grown up in the less-than-affluent section of West Pilton in Edinburgh. He'd go to school wearing three pairs of socks just to fit into his older brother's hand-me-down shoes. His mum worked two jobs and was rarely home. When she was, it was just long enough to put bangers and mash on the table for her sons, then it was out the door again to her second job as a cleaner at the local factory. His father was the parent home more often at the family stead, too unsteady to report to work, but his dark and stormy moods drove ten-year old Jack to prefer he not be. Young Jack had lain nights in bed, worn from playing hard at a game of "catchy" with the neighborhood boys, but would be hard-pressed to fall asleep as the raised voices of his parents drifted up the stairs to his room. It was always about money, or more specifically lack thereof, but regardless, it was not an easy lullaby. Jack would lie awake, staring at the ceiling, listening plaintively to the call of the trains at Pilton Station and desperately wishing one would whisk him away to some far off place and nobler adventure.

Then one day, quite unexpectedly, Jack's mother didn't come home. There were no sausages and potatoes on the table at supper. There were no washed socks to stuff the room in his shoes. Just a book on his bed stand inscribed with a note. "I'm off to find a better place. I'll send for you and your brother when I do. You'll always be my greatest treasure."

The book was *Treasure Island*, and Jack read it cover to cover while he waited for his mother to send for him. He read it again while he sat on the stoop waiting for the post that was sure to bring her letter. He read it again over the months that past when he no longer needed the socks to fill the void in his shoes. He read it again when his older brother went off to University to study archaeology. He even read it years later at his father's bedside as the man passed from complications of the liver.

Jack envied Jim Hawkins, his adventures on the open seas, the strange family the boy had gathered about himself with Squire Trelawney, Captain Smollett, and the irascible Long John Silver.

But mostly, he envied Hawkins the gold. If he had had but a fraction of Flint's gold, young Jack thought, perhaps his mother would have stayed. She would not have left her boys and gone off in search of fortunes elsewhere.

Here, then, was the root of Jack's obsession with treasure. He became a self-made man. From the bridge that was his boardroom, he raided other companies with the ferocity of a blood-thirsty buccaneer, brandishing his power like a cutlass. Then he used his vast fortunes to finance treasure-hunting exhibitions across the globe, much to his advisors dismay. But Jack would not be dissuaded. Nothing would stand between him and the gold. Not work. Not friends. Not family. He eventually abandoned them all in pursuit of the accumulated wealth and valuable objects of lost civilizations, ancient kingdoms, and deposed rulers of the past. Gold was security. But it was never enough. The fever burned hot, and nothing would cool his fevered brow.

Then came the letter.

CHAPTER THIRTEEN

Going On Account

Smout lay in bed, staring at the ceiling. The alarm clock on his bedside table ticked the hour on toward midnight. The full moon shone brightly through his window, making the bedroom nearly bright as daylight. Yet, that was not what was keeping Smout awake. He held Uncle Bernie's dominoes in his hand, clicking them together as he thought over his uncle's warning message: DANGER.

What danger, Smout thought. Did this have

something to do with his uncle's disappearance? And he still didn't know what the piece of map was for. He continued to click the dominoes.

Miss Dumbarton had surprised the children as they heatedly discussed their plan of action. They were all to report to school the next day, and they were no closer to unraveling the meaning of Uncle Bernie's message. Before they had found an answer, Miss Dumbarton ushered Smout upstairs to wash immediately and shooed the remaining children out the front door. Then, she planted herself firmly in the downstairs parlor between Smout and any possible path of escape.

With a heavy sigh, Smout had plodded off to the bath, and then to bed.

"And don't forget to wash behind your ears!" Miss Dumbarton had ordered. "There's enough dirt back there to plant cabbages! In fact, I think I even see a bit of cabbage leaf."

Smout had, indeed, pulled a piece of wilted green vegetation from behind his right ear, a remnant of the day's earlier food fight.

Now, ears scrubbed, face washed, and teeth brushed, he lie awake in bed, puzzling the matter alone. He sat upright and reached for the small canvas bag from which Bogey had first dumped the dominoes. He turned it over in his palm. It was a plain bag. No lettering. No tag to indicate its origins. Just an anonymous canvas sack with a drawstring. His left hand wandered over a small lump in the sack. Had they missed something? Excitedly, he turned the bag inside-out. A small scrap of torn paper dropped out. Smout grabbed his glasses from the nightstand. He eagerly unfolded the slip of paper.

It was another piece of the map!

Yellowed as the first scrap, this piece, too, contained the curving line of coastal waters. Scrawled across the surface were foreign names, locations like "Hautbowline Head" and "Mazenmast Hill." Even stranger still were the familiar words like "skeleton," "foul ground," and "swamp." But the words that made Smout's eyes grow wide, the ones that made his jaw fall slack were written in blood red ink next to a bold, crimson cross.

"Bulk of treasure here," Smout whispered. The paper scrap fluttered to the ground.

"Well, of course you need to tell the police," Emma stated. "This could have everything to do with your uncle's disappearance." It was the next morning and the group of children gathered outside the rector's office awaiting their appointed assignment.

"Are you mad?" Mad Dog spluttered. "It's a treasure map! You tell those bumble-headed twits about it, and we'll never get a crack at the gold."

Several fourth-year girls walking by turned curious heads in their direction.

Rory flashed a brilliant I'm-the-star-athlete-of-the-school grin at them and they giggled shyly as they scurried away. He shushed Mad Dog with a fervent wave of his hand.

"Keep it down, will you? If there's one way for sure to let the secret out, it's to let a girl hear about it," he grumbled. Emma rolled her eyes. Rory smiled ruefully.

"No offense," he muttered.

"But we've no idea what the clue on the back even means!" Bogey whined.

"Let's have another look," Rory suggested. Smout discreetly pulled the new scrap of map from his right trouser pocket.

"The key is the key? What's that about? And what's this here? A bit of music?" Mad Dog bullied his way forward to catch a better glimpse of the clue in Smout's hand. Scrawled above the cryptic clue, six dots and a lowercase "r" danced a little hill across five straight lines. As for its meaning, the children remained puzzled.

"Well, it's certainly not safe for us to go mucking about ourselves. You all saw the warning message," Emma cautioned.

"Yeah," Bogey said. "Danger. But danger from what? Or who?"

"I've no idea," Smout began. "But if Uncle Bernie thought the police could help, why didn't he send this map to them? Why did he send it to me?" He searched their blank faces for answers, but saw nothing there.

"It's settled then. We're the ones to find this treasure. My Uncle Bernie is the only family I have left. If finding the rest of this map and the treasure helps me get him back, then I don't care if things get a little dangerous. Besides, what's the worst that could happen, right?"

Suddenly, the door to the rector's office opened and Smout fell smartly on his bottom.

The iron cell door echoed with the finality of a death knell. Bernie McManus waited until his captor disappeared down a narrow corridor before he moved toward the iron tray holding his meager dinner. He nudged the cold peas that seemed to fluoresce an unappetizing green even in the dim lantern light. There was a slab of dull brown buried under a lump of congealed gravy. Bernie supposed it could have been meat. He sighed. How long had he been down here? Moreover, how long did they intend to keep him here? Besides the odd little Spaniard and the robot, he had seen no one else. He hoped frantically that did not mean Smout was now the prey. His head dropped between his knees.

Bernie had lost track of the time. With no window to mark the sunrise and sunset, he was uncertain if it had been mere days, or had time already stretched into weeks? When he'd first awoke in the dank stone cell, he had tried to discover a means of escape. He scrabbled at the stone walls. He had worried at the key lock of the imposing iron cell door, searching for a weakness, but to no avail. He had cried out into the deepening darkness until he was hoarse, but no one came.

He pushed the food tray away, disgusted, and leaned heavily into the cold wall. As his eyes wandered over the face of the opposite wall, it was clear he was not the first occupant of the cell. Ancient signatures, some dating back to the 1600s, were etched there, silent witness to prisoners past. Some flowed in surprisingly ornate script, while some were chiseled in simple juxtaposing lines. There were even some crude artistic renderings, awkward patterns drawn in the reluctant stone.

As a prisoner in the castle, Bernie knew he shared a fraternity with many men. Some great. Some common. Some dastardly. Some even quite daring like the infamous men of the pirate ship, *The Eagle*.

Bernie smiled ruefully as he thought on Captain Walter Kennedy's ship and the nineteen men captured off the Scottish coast of Argyll. The pirate crew was clapped in irons and escorted by a heavily armed dragoon to Edinburgh Castle where they were imprisoned in the dungeons. Tried for their crimes against the Crown, most were tarred and hung at Leith, between the high and low water marks, a dire warning to others who might be tempted by the siren call of adventure on the open seas and treasure.

Ironic now, then, that it was the hunt for treasure that was responsible for Bernie's current predicament. It was not pirate gold he sought, however. It was the gold of the Jacobites, six caskets of Louis d'Ors. Gold sent to support Bonnie Prince Charlie in his attempts to regain the Scottish throne. But the clandestine delivery had been betrayed, and the gold secreted away, lost to history, waiting to be discovered.

Yet someone had discovered it, Bernie believed. Someone who treasured adventure far more than any sum. Someone who then set about creating the greatest adventure of all and Bernie had been hot on his heels.

Now, Bernie thought as he surveyed his prison cell, he could only hope that wee Smout was adventurer enough to pick up the scent and follow the trail to its amazing end.

CHAPTER FOURTEEN

The Limping Man

Fear had stolen the children's voices. It hadn't helped that the day had dawned, grey and miserable. A biting rain tore at the morning, bent on attacking every dry spot from Old Town to Leith. Menacing clouds cloaked the sun, roiling in dark anger as they unleashed their insistent cargo.

The children braved the damp, dodging puddles, and now they sat, huddled together, in the rector's office, staring at the huge figure towering before them. It was as if a humorous god had upheaved the Ben from the Lochaber highlands and plopped the mountain on the Oriental rug in front of the rector's desk. The man's craggy face itself could have been carved from stone as it betrayed not a twitch, not a hint of movement, not even when Bogey warily fished a particularly juicy one from his right nostril and smeared it under his seat.

The threads on the silent leviathan's grey silk suit stretched to their maximum across his broad, muscled chest. A fly buzzed across his face, level with the two dark lines of brow that knit together across the bridge of his nose. Yet, he made no move to dismiss it.

The door to the outer office flew open and the rector scurried in followed closely by Dunleavey. The thin secretary drew a sharp intake of breath as he nearly collided with the colossus in the grey suit.

"Well, well, well," the rector began. "I see we are all here. Good, good, good."

He sat behind his desk, fussing with the stacks of paper on his desk until all the edges were neatly squared off.

"It seems a fortuitous opportunity has presented itself. First off, I must say, the Academy enjoys the graciousness of a great many benefactors. Indeed, it is through their generosity that we can successfully continue our operation to cultivate such fine young minds."

Mad Dog's knuckles cracked like gunfire in response. The rector sighed heavily before continuing.

"Of course, in some cases we are more successful than others." The rector reprimanded Mad Dog with a stern gaze.

"As I was saying, we owe much to these generous donors. Now, it seems one such donor has taken an interest in you sorry lot. He believes he has a project that will fulfill your service obligations and build some fortitude of character. Mr. Dunleavey, of course, will tag along as chaperone, and Mr. Grey here will escort you to your destination." Dunleavey gulped audibly.

Rory leaned in to Emma. "Straight to the graveyard, most likely. Check the size of that chap's arms. They're bigger 'round than the Mons Meg cannon!"

Emma nodded nervously in agreement. Smout squeezed her hand. "Don't worry, Emma," Smout whispered. "I'll protect you."

She managed a weak smile. They all looked back at the rector as he continued.

"Very well. Off with you then. I expect you all to be on your best behavior. Make Edinburgh Academy proud!"

The round little rector waved them from the room. They gathered their belongings and shuffled after the stoic Mr. Grey.

They made a funny little caravan as they walked though the school, drawing looks from the blue-jacketed students milling about between classes. The silent giant in the suit took point. Rory and Emma followed a cautious number of paces behind. Mad Dog plodded along with his caveman gait. Bogey skipped carelessly just in front the nail-chewing Dunleavey.

"Oh, I'm not certain about this," Dunleavey

prattled to no one in particular. "No, not certain at all. What was the rector thinking, sending me along? Chaperone indeed! That brute could have me for breakfast and wash me down with a spot of tea!"

Smout was inclined to agree, but kept his thoughts to himself. He straggled behind, clicking the dominoes safely tucked in his trouser pocket. Their silent message echoed ominously in his head.

Danger. Danger. Danger. Then there was the new message he had discovered on the map scrap in the canvas bag. He shuddered.

He stole a glance at the menacing hulk leading the rag tag bunch. Could this man possibly be the danger Uncle Bernie was trying to warn him about, Smout wondered. And who was this mysterious benefactor the rector had mentioned?

Smout nearly ran over Dunleavey as the group came to an abrupt halt. They had reached the street. The rain had temporarily retreated, but the dark clouds remained, threatening to open a deluge once more.

A long black limousine idled at the curb. Mr.

Grey bent down and silently opened the passenger door. There was a moment of uncertainty, an uneasy silence, then Mad Dog let out an excited whoop and dove headfirst into the luxury car. A few seconds passed and his shaggy head popped through the door, his beefy hands stuffed with sweets.

"Have a look! There's chocolate bars and caramel truffles! I think there's even an ice box with fizzies in here! I'm beginning to like this service project. We should have started a food fight ages ago. Come on!" The children exchanged wary glances, then squealed in delight as they piled into the limousine.

Mr. Grey motioned to Dunleavey. The skinny secretary adjusted his satchel and straightened his shoulders as a wide smile spread across his thin face.

"Well, I suppose if one is about to meet a bitter end why not go bravely and in style?" With that, he ducked his lanky frame into the vehicle. Smout hesitated for a moment then joined the others as Mr. Grey shut the door.

The house was handsome, a stately Georgian facing the manicured Queen Street Gardens. Hidden away from the wandering public eye behind rod iron fences and dense hedges, the gardens held their share of green secrets. If you fancied a glimpse from a second story window, you could follow the rippling rings of chickadees and finches as they frolicked in Farmer Woods' cattle pond. Now, the thick foliage of tall trees held the garden's secrets close, open only to those with a key.

The limousine pulled up at the curb. Mr. Grey dutifully stepped out and opened the vehicle door. The children emptied out onto the sidewalk followed by the wiry Dunleavey, who brushed teacake crumbs from his lapel. The secretary's dour mood had improved immensely on the luxurious ride across town.

"Quite a lovely trip, indeed," he prattled to Mr. Grey. "Please, do extend out thanks to your employer. Never have I been escorted in such...," he began, but merely coughed in the cloud of petrol fumes that erupted as the limousine pulled away.

"Well, now, that's just impolite!" Dunleavey muttered.

"Speaking of impolite," he turned to reprimand the children who just moments before had been bursting with the excited energy brought on by sugar-enriched sweets and drinks. Now, however, they were frozen as a unit. They stared up at the blood-red lacquered door at the top of the stairs. A solid brass knocker hung, heavy and ominous, at the center, waiting to rap out the knell of their arrival. An ominous roll of thunder shuddered through the dismal sky.

Mad Dog nudged Bogey with a sharp elbow. "Who do you suppose lives here?"

Bogey flinched from the blow. He rubbed his ribs. "Don't know. Do you suppose Death keeps a flat in Heriot Row?"

A loud laugh burst from Mad Dog, but disappeared as quickly as it sounded.

"Are you complete idiots?" Emma's voice broke the tension with the brutality of a sledgehammer.

"17 Heriot Row?" she continued. The boys blinked stupidly. Emma huffed with as much exasperation as she could muster.

"This is the home of Robert Louis Stevenson! Boys!" She threw her hands up in the air. "Really!"

With that, she jogged up the steps and rapped the knocker smartly.

"Now, how do you suppose she knew that?" Mad Dog asked.

Bogey shrugged. "Women's intuition?"

"Fellas?" Rory gestured to an engraved brick anchored near the door, just above the brass bell.

Smout squinted as he read the letters chiseled into the grey stone. "Home of Robert Louis Stevenson, 1857-1880. Well. What do you know?"

"Women's intuition, huh?" Mad Dog growled as he delivered a smack to the back of Bogey's head. Bogey grinned sheepishly as the lot bounded up the steps to join Emma.

The Stevenson House was not, much to the group's relief, home to Death, or any other spooky spirits. Rather, the historic home was now owned by a delightful family who opened their house to the public as a bed and breakfast and meeting facility. The house had retained much of its original structure and overflowed with antiques, many from Stevenson's era.

Smout gawked in awe, drinking in the details. He'd known, of course, that the childhood home of Stevenson was in Edinburgh. He just hadn't realized how close it was to his own.

As they travelled though the front hall, his eyes drifted up toward the rounded cupola which, in less inclement weather, let in streams of brightening sunshine. He let his gaze wander up the stone staircase where a variety of swords guarded the walls in swashbuckling splendor. Smout fancied they were the sort brandished by the pirates in Stevenson's work.

"Don't touch *anything*!" Dunleavey warned as they were led to the drawing room. Emma pulled her hands back from the delicate china figurine she'd been about to examine on a nearby piano.

"Sit there and don't move," Dunleavey

117

ordered. They wedged themselves, five across, on a narrow chaise, while Dunleavey chose a chintz-covered, well-stuffed armchair for himself. The teacakes had lulled him into a sleepy stupor. He sighed contentedly and soon, settled into a steady snore while they awaited their host.

"Oof! Watch your elbow!" Emma warned.

"I would," Rory grumbled, "but, Genius here has his hand in my face." He fumbled, trying to push Bogey's hand down. Bogey, for his part, was trying to pull his other arm free, seeing that it was currently trapped under Mad Dog's considerable bulk. Smout remained oblivious to the squabbling, his ear trained on another sound echoing from the corridor.

Thump. Drag. Thump. Drag.

Smout stiffened. He listened more intently. He was almost certain. The sound drew even closer.

Thump. Drag. Thump. Drag.

A few more seconds passed, and there could be no doubt. It was the same sound he had heard from the locker!

"Rory!" Smout whispered tersely. "Rory!"

Smout tried desperately to gain the teen's attention, but Rory was too engrossed in his squabbling match with Emma and Bogey. Not to mention, the steady sawing of Dunleavey's snores drowned any hope of Smout's being heard.

Thump. Drag. Thump. Drag.

Smout waved frantically. "Rory!"

Finally, Mad Dog let out an ear-piercing, "Oi!"

Dunleavey sprung aright from his nap, arms flailing. The children froze.

Suddenly the doorway filled with the very incarnation of Long John Silver himself. The crooked nose told tales of back-alley brawls and coarse disagreements. The long, white scar writhed on the mahogany cheek. The blood-scarlet eyes atop the skeleton cane winked as they caught the light.

But all of it paled in comparison to the words they heard next.

"So, who here wants to find a treasure?"

CHAPTER FIFTEEN

Bamboozled

Dunleavey jumped to his feet with all the grace of an awkwardly jointed marionette.

"A treasure hunt? Mr. Bluidy!" he spluttered. Dunleavey struggled between propriety and the urge to call one of the Academy's most generous donors an addle-pated twit.

Fortunately for Dunleavey, Bluidy's hearty chuckle rescued the gawky secretary from a deepening shade of raspberry-plum. He clapped the wiry man between the shoulder blades.

"Calm yourself, Mr. Dunleavey. I was merely sporting. What I have in mind for the children is far-less intriguing and, I'm afraid, a bit more mind-numbing."

The color evened in Dunleavey's cheeks. This sounded like a much more suited and boring activity. Still, the secretary found his eyes darting to Bluidy as the fierce-looking man limped across the room. Boring just didn't seem to describe the man with the scarred face.

Bluidy took a seat across from the children. "The truth of the matter is I am only in Edinburgh for a short time. You see, I plan to make an acquisition of valuable Highland artifacts and am merely in town to close the deal and transport them to my ship at the Port Edgar Marina."

Bogey's head popped up in curiosity. He grasped at the glimmer of excitement. "You have a ship?"

Bluidy nodded. "A Baltic trader, in fact. It's quite useful in navigating around the globe. I am a collector of sorts. Items from all over the world –

Egypt, the Americas – my own personal treasure trove of history."

Smout felt the hairs on the back of his neck stand on end. He was certain his uncle would not like this man. Uncle Bernie believed the past belonged to everyone, not to just one man. It was why he had become curator at the museum, to bring the treasures of the past to the people of the present. As Smout's fingers toyed with the bits of map in his pocket, he couldn't help wondering if his uncle's last quest had run him afoul of a man like Bluidy.

"At any rate, I need to make room on my boat. I am a little short on crew, and could use a few swabs to clear the decks. Your rector mentioned he had a few able bodies, so here we are," Bluidy announced exuberantly.

"Swab decks?" Mad Dog groaned. "Are you serious?"

"Oh, indeed I am. I'll have the car brought 'round and transport you to the docks. I hope you've brought sunscreen. Even with cloud cover the rays can bring a bit of color to your cheeks."

Dunleavey stood. "That sounds positively delightful!"

The children eyed him suspiciously as though he had a third eye sprouting in the middle of his forehead.

"I suppose I should, however, take a moment to check in with the rector. Just to let him know things are shipshape." Tickled at his feeble joke, he giggled like a giddy schoolgirl.

"Of course," Bluidy agreed. "There's a telephone in the room down the hall. After your call, you should take a moment and enjoy the gardens out back. It will give the children and I chance to get acquainted."

At the mention of the word garden, that familiar twitch niggled at Smout's ten-year old brain. His hand reached into his pocket and clacked his uncle's dominoes together. Before his thoughts could congeal, Rory nudged him sharply in the ribs.

"Hey. That's the man I saw in the rector's office. The one reading the article about treasure."

"Makes a chap wonder. What 'artifacts' do

you suppose he's trying to acquire?" Bogey asked.

"Don't know, but I say we don't trust the bugger," Mad Dog offered.

"I can't believe I'm about to say this," Emma began, "but, I think Mad Dog's right."

Mad Dog's eyes popped open in surprise. The harsh line of his mouth broke into a wide grin. Emma shook her head.

"Don't get used to it," she warned. Mad Dog nodded intensely.

"'Course not," he replied.

"Yes," Bluidy continued, blathering to Mr. Dunleavey. "Life here in Heriot Row had a great influence on Mr. Stevenson. It inspired his famous poem *The Lamplighter*."

"For we are very lucky, with a lamp before the door, and Leerie stops to light it as he lights so many more!" Emma recited. "I know that poem! It's from Stevenson's *A Child's Garden of Verses*."

"Top marks to you, Miss Johnson. That's exactly right," Bluidy responded before he returned to waxing eloquent on the house's many historical points. Dunleavey's head nodded and bobbled in appreciation.

An idea clicked in Smout's brain. He leapt forward, electrified with purpose. He motioned quickly for the rest of the children to huddle around the coffee table. Glancing over his shoulder, making certain the adults were otherwise occupied, he scrambled to lay out the dominoes in a six-letter pattern.

"What gives?" Rory whispered.

"The letters. Look at the letters," Smout urged. "They spell something."

"'Course they do!" Mad Dog muttered. "We already figured that out, you twit! They spell danger."

Smout shook his head. "No. We only assumed they spelled danger, but look! If you rearrange them like this, see? They spell out G-A-R-D-E-N."

He was met with four blank stares. He sighed before he launched into an explanation. "The first clue led us to *Treasure Island*. 'Only Blind Pew can read Billy's Bones.'"

"What if this clue," he began, pointing to the dominoes, "was meant to lead us to *A Child's Garden of Verses?*"

Rory shook his head. "What are you getting at, Smout?"

"What if all the clues have something to do with Robert Louis Stevenson? Uncle Bernie knows he's my favorite author. What better place to leave his clues?"

Mad Dog didn't bother to stifle his guffaw. "You're barking mad, little man."

The room had suddenly fallen into an eerie silence. Smout looked over his shoulder. Dunleavey was nowhere to be found.

"Oh, but that sounds like a fine idea to me." A low, guttural voice startled the children into a frozen silence.

He didn't like people. Since he was a child, soft around the middle with his lazy eye drooping over his wide, flat nose, they poked fun at him and called him names like *gordito*. Even when he helped the pretty girls with their school work, they refused to acknowledge his existence when they were in public. They ignored him in favor of the richer boys, the more handsome boys. They wanted nothing to do with the poor little fat boy who helped them pass their lessons.

No, you couldn't make people do what you wanted them to do, no matter how hard you tried. But, robots? Robots were a different story.

When he created a robot, Arturo Sandoval imagined he understood what it felt like to be a god. He could take a lifeless hunk of metal and wire and create a moveable body structure, a delicate sensory system, and through no small miracle, could breathe electronic life into a brain that told the systems what to do, what *he* wanted it to do. In short, he created a race of beings that worshipped him and only him, their electronic deity.

He wasn't, of course, the only scientist in the world creating artificial life. Japan had its toy robotic dogs and strange, spaceman-like humanoid automatons. NASA, of course, had its Mars rovers exploring the mystery of the Red Planet. But none of them came close to the brilliance that was his *Piratino*.

When he first conceived the idea of the odd little robot, penciled renderings of solenoid actuators and pneumatic systems that would make his creation move, it was merely a dream on paper. Then the knock came on his door and his mysterious benefactor introduced himself. The man had read some of his articles in an obscure scientific journal discussing how his robot design could be used to find anything underground - missing corpses, buried landmines...treasure. To the respected scientific community, it was madness to assume the proposed radar technology on Sandoval's robot could find anything more than a needle in a haystack, but the strange man on his doorstep had seemed mad. Mad with the need to find gold. He had provided Sandoval with all the funding he had needed and the means to rise above all the beautiful people who had snubbed him over the years. They would fawn over him and worship at his feet.

He *would* be a god.

But, first, he had to find the treasure.

The boom of the One O'Clock gun shuddered through the roots of the Castle, shaking Sandoval from his reverie. Time was running short. Few ventured down as deep into the Castle's bowels, the oldest and darkest furrows, that housed the dank dungeon cells like the one McManus currently occupied. Even fewer were aware of the secret tunnel that ran beneath the Royal Mile, connecting the Castle with Holyrood Palace. But preparations were beginning for Edinburgh's world-renowned Military Tattoo. That meant tighter security. And a ticking clock.

Soon performers and visitors from all over the world would converge on Edinburgh to share performances of some of their greatest national treasures. The squat, little man scoffed. The only treasure he was interested in glittered.

He waddled to the bars on McManus' cell. "You think you are clever, sending clues to the

129

treasure's location to your young nephew."

Bernie started at the mention of young Smout. The madman must have seen him put the package in the post. The scientist leered.

"You see? Your emotions give you away. But, do not worry. As long as he cooperates with my employer, no harm will come to his pretty little head."

Bernie's eyes narrowed as the gravity of the statement bore down upon him.

"Yes, Mr. McManus. There is a wolf among the lambs. An enemy sailing under a false flag. My employer is with your nephew and his friends as we speak. Soon, we will have everything we need to find Prince Charlie's lost gold. Then," the Spaniard paused for effect, "then we will have no need of you."

CHAPTER SIXTEEN

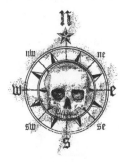

Flotsam & Jetsam

MacIntosh sat heavily in his desk chair and expelled a whoosh of exasperated air that fluttered the ends of his bushy mustache. He reached both hands up and ran them through wild Einsteinian hair that was feathered through with premature grey. Heavy lids closed over his bright blue eyes as his arms stretched high and his hands interlaced behind his head. He just needed to think. His gut told him they were missing something about this business. Witness statements and forensic facts could point you in the right direction on a case, but the seasoned veteran knew when to trust gut instinct, and the feeling in the pit of his stomach growled past his noontime neeps and tatties to tell him something was rotten in the state of Denmark.

Meanwhile, Scribbles typed up notes at a nearby station. Unlike his superior officer, he kept his dark brown hair cropped high and tight and was less likely to build a case based simply on mild indigestion.

Their names weren't really MacIntosh and Scribbles, of course, though they very well should have been. Detective Inspector Angus Markham rarely stepped from the police offices on Fettes Avenue without his drab trenchcoat, regardless of the weather. Perhaps he'd watched one too many American detective shows as a lad, or read too many pulp novels about secretive spies, but the long-legged, middle-aged inspector always wore his crumpled coat, come rain or come shine.

Scribbles, or rather, Detective Sergeant Jaimie MacGregor, cut a more tailored figure than the older man. The lines of his suit were crisp. The crease in his pants, sharp. For MacGregor, it was all about the details. He could always be found with pen in hand, writing furiously in his anonymous little notebook. At a crime scene, he jotted down facts and minutiae that often helped the police solve puzzling cases. Sometimes, however, when Inspector Markham droned on about police policy and proper procedure, he just doodled random little pictures in the margins. He was particularly proud of his sketch of Markham in his signature coat, wearing ridiculously large clown shoes and a wild, curly-topped wig. He did worry that one day his superior might find the drawing and be chuffed. But at the moment, Inspector Markham seemed more upset by the case of the missing museum curator.

"This case is driving me batty, MacGregor!" Markham bellowed as he flipped a file closed.

MacGregor glanced up, his expert fingers still clacking away at the computer keyboard. "Why's that, Inspector?"

"It makes no bloody sense! This McManus

fellow. What's his first name? Bernard? Well, I can't, for the life of me, understand why anyone would want to make him disappear. I've been looking over his dossier. He used to be at the top of his game. Made some major finds as an archaeologist. That's how he got his post as curator of the museum. Lately though, he spends his days cataloguing old bones and dinosaur droppings. Dreadfully boring stuff. Nothing worth kidnapping a person over."

"Sounds like," MacGregor agreed. He looked up from his computer screen. "He's probably sticking closer to home for his nephew's sake. Poor kid's had rotten luck."

"How's that?" Markham leaned forward, one crazy salt-and-pepper eyebrow raised.

"Here. Have a look." MacGregor pointed to the screen as Markham circled round the desk. "Seems his father and his mother both disappeared under mysterious circumstances. They were both archaeologists, too. Hey! Maybe it's like the Curse of Tutankhamen. You remember all those chaps died after entering Tut's tomb? The inscription warned them. 'Death shall come upon swift wings to him who violates this tomb.'"

MacGregor pointed at the photo of the trio on his screen. They looked chummy with arms wrapped around each other's shoulders. "Maybe the lot of them dug up some cursed mummy's grave, or the like."

Markham waved him off like an annoying fly. "Codswallop! There's no such thing!"

MacGregor couldn't resist. "Say what you will, but eight people died within twelve years of opening that tomb."

"Yet Howard Carter, the expedition's leader, lived to be sixty-four! It's all legend and hooey!"

MacGregor could barely conceal his grin as Markham stomped back to his desk. Sometimes it was just too easy. MacGregor looked at the photo again. His keen eyes roved over the picture, dissecting details and storing them in his agile memory. The trio looked as though they were enjoying themselves immensely. Large smiles plastered across their faces, even though the tropical palms and stretching sand behind them suggested they were miles from civilized society. MacGregor scanned the caption.

"Archaeological team makes historic find on Juan Fernandez Archipelago." Hm, MacGregor thought. South America.

He continued to peruse the photo. Someone had pitched a canvas tent in the background. The lot of them resembled bedraggled, drowned rats in scuba gear as they stood over a collection of pottery shards and barnacle-encrusted junk. Whatever did they have to be so blasted happy about? To MacGregor's unschooled eye, it looked like so much flotsam and jetsam. He shrugged. One man's trash is another man's treasure, he thought.

The two men in the photograph were as different as night and day. The man on the left was tall and broad. An intricate diver's watch with numerous dials and buttons stretched across the sinewy muscles of his left wrist. His dark, wet hair tightened in ringlets around a long face with dark eyes. Duncan McManus, Smout's father.

MacGregor checked the dates. Duncan McManus went missing on this very trip. Curious.

He looked at the others in the photo. Bernard McManus stood a full head shorter than his brother. His light brown hair fell longer and straighter than his younger sibling's.

The young woman in between them was slight, a fair-haired pixie with blonde hair. Her damp hair was a tangled, matted mess trapped under her diving mask, but Victoria McManus' blue eyes danced, as if she had found the world's most spectacular treasure instead of a pile of scrap. Hard to picture anyone wanting to inflict harm on such a happy lot. Yet, the three people in this photo were all missing, leaving behind one small, lonely boy...and a trail of mystery.

CHAPTER SEVENTEEN

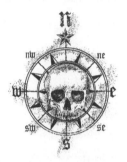

A Pirate Story

It was no mystery. The boy held the key to finding the bulk of Charlie's gold. Bluidy was certain of it. If he couldn't win the children over soon, however, he feared he would have to take more drastic measures. He was not the only interested party pursuing Charlie's lost gold. And while he had his reasons for not wanting to harm young Smout, the others endeavoring to find the massive treasure would not think twice about eliminating any obstacles. That included Smout and his young friends.

But, some secrets were better kept to oneself. He would let the children know only what they needed to know. That was all. He needed to proceed carefully, but quickly.

Bluidy took up residence in the chintz armchair recently vacated by Dunleavey. His hands crossed over the crown of his skeleton cane. They were not the hands of a rich businessman. Rather, they were rough and heavily calloused, like hands that had toiled for endless hours at some driving task in weather fair and weather foul. He raised the long index finger and tapped a steady rhythm. Smout shuddered as he realized Bluidy's tapping paced his own pulse, beat for beat, almost as if he could sense the racing impulses of his heart, like they were...connected in some way. Bluidy leaned in toward the children.

"You look like a smart lot. What do you know about Scottish history, hm?" he asked.

Bogey chuckled. "I know it puts me to sleep quicker than a warm glass of milk."

Bluidy smiled. "I can appreciate that. But,

what if I were to tell you a story about a plot to steal a throne, a bloody battle, a prince in disguise, and a king's ransom in gold?"

With each word that trickled from Bluidy's mouth, the cloak of apprehension fell from their shoulders, and the boys scooted nearer the edge of their seat. Emma merely rolled her eyes, but settled back, nonetheless, into the chaise to listen to Bluidy's tale.

He began his story in 1720, when Prince Charles Edward Stuart, one of the last legitimate heirs to the House of Stuart, was born. His family had ruled Scotland until 1689 when a revolution deposed the Stuarts, denying them the Crown. In 1745, in a campaign to take back the throne he believed to be his, Bonnie Prince Charlie marched on Edinburgh with the Jacobites and successfully defeated the Hanoverian army at the Battle of Prestopans.

"Maybe he wasn't such a nancy boy after all," Bogey interrupted. He was met with a rash of bewildered stares.

"Nevermind," he muttered.

"Unfortunately, that's where Charlie's successes ended," Bluidy continued. He went on to describe Charlie's defeat at the Battle of Culloden and his forced exile, disguising himself as a lady's maidservant to escape pursuers.

"Nope. I was right. Nancy boy," Bogey mumbled. Rory smacked Bogey's head.

Then Bluidy began the most intriguing part of his tale.

"It took time for news of Charlie's defeat to reach the ears of his supporters. Before his French allies caught wind, they sent two frigates, packed with seven casks of gold, now worth nearly £5 million, to Scottish shores. And that's when the gold mysteriously disappears, lost for centuries. That is, until now," Bluidy concluded.

The children exchanged anxious glances. Smout felt his hand drift again to the scraps of map secreted away in his pocket. Could their map possibly lead to Prince Charlie's treasure?

"You've discovered the location of Prince Charles' gold?" Emma asked.

"Not exactly." Bluidy stood, moving near the fireplace, and rested a long arm on the mantle. "But I believe someone did."

The children, already balanced precariously on the edge of the chaise, now leaned even further forward, waiting for Bluidy to reveal the anonymous someone.

"Who?" they asked in unison.

Bluidy turned to face the children, a fevered look burning in his eyes.

"Why, the man who penned perhaps the greatest buried treasure story of all time, of course." Bluidy pointed to a portrait hanging serenely on the wall. The children turned to see the long, gaunt face of the man who had once lived in the very house they now occupied. Robert Louis Stevenson.

CHAPTER EIGHTEEN

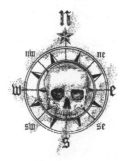

Freebooter

"Robert Louis Stevenson? A treasure hunter? Do you honestly expect us to believe you?" Emma asked.

Bluidy reclaimed his seat, crossing his legs at the ankles. "Honestly? No. Not without a bit of proof, at any rate."

The children exchanged glances. What proof could Bluidy offer? Once again, Smout's hand drifted toward his pocket.

"Proof? Like what?" Mad Dog growled.

A heavy thunk echoed on the coffee table in front of the children. Their eyes immediately pulled to the wildly spinning orb that twirled there. The golden dervish spun till gravity won out and it rung to a glittering halt on the polished pine surface. A sudden shimmering excitement flushed the cheeks of the group as they leaned over the glittering gold coin that lay just within their reach.

"Is that what I think it is?" Bogey whispered.

Emma nodded breathlessly. "A Louis d'Or!"

Mad Dog wrinkled his brow. He scratched his shaggy mane of hair. "Or? Or what?"

Bluidy grinned. "No, my young friend. 'Or' is the French word for 'gold'."

"Caw! Why can't you blokes just say 'treasure'?" Mad Dog crowed. "All these code words and secrets and bits of map," he began. At mention of the word map, Bluidy raised a curious eyebrow. Rory rewarded Mad Dog with a sharp elbow in the ribs. The children were not quite ready to trust the rough man.

"Oof!" Mad Dog grunted. If Bluidy noticed

the jab, he did not let on. He limped toward the piano nestled in the corner of the room. His rough fingers picked out a clumsy tune. Emma took the opportunity to change the subject.

"Do you play, Mr. Bluidy?" Emma asked.

Bluidy shook his head and hands vigorously. "No, no, no. I never had the grace and skill to become an accomplished pianist. That talent, I'm afraid, fell to my wife. She was the musician in the family."

Bogey cocked his head sideways, trying to picture the rough, fierce man living commuting from Comely Bank, kissing an apron-clad missus on the cheek as he dutifully travelled to a sedate desk job in some cubicle.

"Somebody married you?" Bogey cracked. The impolite comment earned him another smart smack from Rory. Bluidy chuckled deeply but something else nibbled at the corners of the apparent mirth.

"No, I'm afraid your young friend is quite smart. It was an extraordinary surprise that anyone would accept a marriage proposal from someone like me, but then she was an extraordinary woman."

As Emma sighed casting a longing gaze at Rory, he scooped up the round coin, scowling fiercely as if that would help him ascertain its authenticity and value. Mad Dog and Bogey jockeyed around him, jostling each other like mad pinballs in a frantic effort to see the coin better.

Smout remained silent, sitting deep in thought. He had recognized the look on Bluidy's face. It was the look of a person who had lost someone. Smout knew that feeling all too well. It sort of made him feel like tossing his cookies. Maybe he had something in common with Bluidy after all.

His chest tightened as it suddenly became difficult to breathe, like trying to draw a breath across sandpaper. Smout fished his inhaler from his pocket, his hand brushing the strange pieces of map, and took two brief puffs of medicine. His airways opened and soothing oxygen flowed once more.

"You know, Stevenson himself was a bit of a musician. Composed a great many pieces for the flageolet."

Smout started. He quickly stole a glance at the back of the second piece of map.

Five lines. Seven notes. Could it be one of Stevenson's flageolet melodies? He stuffed the scrap back into his pocket.

On the other side of the room, Rory held the coin up to the light. The face of the coin displayed the profile of Louis XV, the French monarch who at the tender age of five succeeded the famous Sun King to the throne.

On the flip side of the coin, a regal crown hovered over two oval shields. One shield bore the three fleur-de-lis of France, the other, the eight radiating spokes of Navarre's coat of arms. Embossed Latin letters encircled both sides of the coin. The reverse side bore the date 1745.

"1745?" Rory turned to Bluidy.

"*Bliadhna Theàrlaich*," Bluidy replied in Scottish Gaelic. "Charles' year."

"Charles? As in Bonnie Prince Charlie, then?" Bogey queried. Bluidy nodded. Bogey's

147

mouth dropped open in a silent "O".

"Bonnie Prince Charlie's gold," Mad Dog murmured as he plucked the coin from Rory, hefting it in his hand, weighing the history that came with it. He raised his shaggy head and narrowed his eyes at Bluidy.

"Where did you get it?" Mad Dog asked, suspicious.

A wide grin broke across Bluidy's face, dividing the plane across his thick scar.

"Why, where every decent freebooting pirate gets his treasure, of course. I stole it."

Few things struck fear into the heart of Detective Inspector Angus Markham. He was a steeled law enforcement officer of over twenty years. He had seen acts of terror. He had been involved in a harrowing stand-off with larcenous bank robbers. He had even endured holiday shopping with his mother-in-law. But if anything in the world curled his toes and set his heart aquiver, it was spiders.

It wasn't a full-fledged phobia. He didn't

mind the small brown house spiders that took up residence next to the pruning shears in his garden shed, but when their leg-span crested more than ten-inches, it was an issue.

Perhaps that was the reason he was examining the far side of Bernie McManus' office, the side furthest from the glass box that housed the most enormous arachnid Markham had ever seen. He couldn't rationalize how any sane person could possibly be brave enough to be in the same room with that creature long enough to have caused the mess through which he was currently sifting.

It looked as though a hurricane had ravaged the office. Papers littered every surface of room, some ringed with circular tan stains. Most likely from countless cups of tea drunk over long hours of inquiry. Stacks of research works, leather-bound in a rainbow of colors, lay open to various pages, dog-eared for ready reference at some later date. An apple browned into over-ripeness, one side caving to decay, hinted at the last time the owner of the office had studied at the wide oak desk in the center of the room.

Markham prodded it with the end of his pen to read the stained paper beneath it. He looked over at his young partner.

"You'd better leave that thing alone. It might eat your face off."

Jaimie MacGregor tapped at the glass of the aquarium where the large, hairy-legged tarantula slowly made its way toward the glass over a rough edged rock.

"*Theraphosa blondi*," a reedy voice called from the doorway currently barricaded by bright yellow crime scene tape. A thin young man in glasses and an argyle sweater vest hovered behind the tape. "Also known as the Goliath Birdeater and they don't usually harm humans. They prefer cockroaches."

He pushed his glasses up as he rattled a clear jar of the six-legged creatures. Markham shuddered as the young man continued. Cockroaches weren't high on his list either.

"She's just responding to the vibrations on the glass. It's how they sense their prey. She's probably just hungry."

Markham pulled MacGregor back. He did not want to test whether the blond-haired spider would enjoy his young partner for lunch.

"I came to feed her. With Dr. McManus gone, I'm the only one who will go near her," the young man continued.

"Rightly so. And you are?" Markham queried.

"Oh, of course. My name's Black. Kieran Black," he shifted the jar of roaches to his left hand and extended his right to shake the Inspector's. Markham grimaced, but shook the young man's outstretched hand then discreetly wiped his own on his trouser leg.

"I'm Dr. McManus' assistant. A student at the University," Black continued. "May I come in?"

Markham nodded. "Yes, but try not to disturb anything."

He gestured to the general disarray around the room. MacGregor offered a withering, sarcastic look. Markham exhaled in exasperation.

151

"Well, at least try not to disturb it more than it already has been."

Black nodded. "Certainly. Certainly."

He ducked under the yellow tape and quickly made his way to the tarantula's enclosure. MacGregor continued to survey the room.

"So, you're obviously aware that the curator is missing?" Markham posed it more as a question. Kieran nodded.

"Oh, yes. The entire staff is quite upset about it. Such a terrible thing." He lifted the screen from the top of the spider enclosure. Markham took several cautious steps backward.

MacGregor grinned then turned his attention back to the odd, scrawled list he had just discovered on McManus' desk. It was a series of numbers and letters, almost like a bowl of alphabet soup.

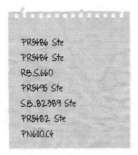

He pulled out his black notebook and began scribbling.

Markham shifted uncomfortably, and cleared his throat. "Do you have any idea what Dr. McManus may have been working on? Anything unusual or dangerous that may have put him at risk?"

Black turned, puzzlement flooding his face. He had picked up the ten-inch spider, letting it crawl over his arm and hand. Markham cringed.

"Dangerous?" Black responded, oblivious to the policeman's discomfort. "No. But, come to think of it, he had been awfully excited about something of late."

He strode toward Inspector Markham, still carrying the large arachnid. "Here. Hold Tina."

He placed the spider on the shoulder of Markham's trench coat. MacGregor stifled a chuckle as he stepped aside to allow Black to search the desk.

Markham's normally deep baritone squeaked in soprano. "Really? What might that have been?"

Nervous perspiration began to bead on the Inspector's forehead as Black rifled through the papers on McManus' desk. As the policeman's growing phobia urged thoughts of early retirement, another sobering thought flitted through his fevered brain. As the room began to swim, he wondered if the hungry spider could feel the vibrating pulse of his panicking heart and might mistake him for a tasty lunch, regardless of what Mr. Black purported.

"Dr. McManus was trying to authenticate something. A letter, I believe. I don't know what it concerned, but he was quite keyed up about it."

Markham responded barely above a whisper as the spider's long legs tickled at his neck. "I completely understand."

"I know he made some notes. If I could just find them...," he trailed off.

Markham swallowed hard. The spider's foreleg explored the hairs inside his ear. "Hurry."

MacGregor fought through a fit of giggles as he watched his superior officer gingerly attempt to wiggle out of his trench coat.

"Do you know if he succeeded in the authentication?" MacGregor asked Black.

"No, but it might be with his notes. I just can't seem to find them," Black offered.

"I would imagine it might be difficult, what with all this mess. Looks like somebody really tossed the place. Maybe they took the notes," MacGregor suggested.

"No one tossed the place," Black stated. "Dr. McManus' office always looks like this."

"I see," MacGregor replied. "May I ask you what you make of this?"

He showed Black the odd alphanumeric listings.

"Library reference numbers, by the look of it. Dr. McManus was forever looking up research to check facts and establish provenance on pieces he was authenticating."

"Provenance? MacGregor asked.

"Origin, or ownership. Where something came from," Black explained.

MacGregor nodded, pocketing his notebook. He made a mental note to check the list. Perhaps the books on the list would shed some light on what

McManus was up to. He turned to Markham, who by now had completely shrugged out from his coat. It now lay draped across the sofa, the curious spider crawling its way up the backrest.

"You ready to go, sir?" MacGregor asked. Markham was already striding for the door.

"Indeed. Thank you for your assistance, Mr. Black. We may be contacting you for further information."

Black nodded as he hurried to the sofa to retrieve Tina. The two policemen quickly made their way out of the museum.

"Sir?" MacGregor questioned. "Aren't you going to retrieve your coat?"

"No. I'd be feeling that creepy crawly all over me every time I'd wear it. I've been meaning to make a change, anyway. Perhaps a nice gabardine."

MacGregor thought about poking fun at his superior officer, but thought better of it. Instead, he shared a piece of information that he'd withheld from Black.

"There's something I didn't mention to

McManus' assistant. There was something else written on the bottom of that list."

MacGregor froze in his tracks. He turned to his young partner.

"What?"

"An address. 42 Henderson Row, Edinburgh, EH3 5 BL. Edinburgh Academy," MacGregor responded.

Markham sucked in a sharp breath. "The boy."

CHAPTER NINETEEN

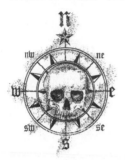

Man-O-War

The sights of Edinburgh passed outside the tinted limousine window as they crawled through the unusually high traffic. They'd had to cut over to Princes Street in an effort to circumvent the gnarl of vehicles congesting the road, locals and visitors vying for space on the streets and avenues. The traffic always swelled during the days before and during Edinburgh's internationally famous Tattoo.

Smout stared blankly as they passed the linear wedge of tan that was the Royal Scottish Academy, perched high on The Mound, that artificial hill that separated Edinburgh's Old Town and New Town. The grey edifice of Edinburgh Castle peeked over the top of the late summer green of West Princes Street Gardens. Through the back window, in the distance, the dark spire of St. Giles Cathedral stretched toward a cerulean blue midday sky. It was a delightful day to be free from school.

Smout could not have cared less.

He was riding in the car with a thief! An honest-to-goodness, low-down, dirty, rotten pirate!

He looked across the cab of the limousine where Bluidy was chatting quite amicably with Mr. Dunleavey. For a moment, Smout swore the skull atop Bluidy's cane winked at him. He shook his head.

They had waited for Bluidy to explain his abrupt confession, but Secretary Dunleavey had inconveniently returned to the parlor before any explanation was given. The children immediately converged upon their chaperone, clamoring in an incoherent babble of voices trying to warn Dunleavey of what Bluidy had just revealed. The skinny secretary had waved his arms, trying to calm the cacophony.

"Settle down! Settle down! What in the world are you talking about?"

Smout pressed forward to answer the question. "He's a rotten thief! He's stolen a piece of the lost gold of Bonnie Prince Charlie!"

Dunleavey looked baffled as Smout shot a withering look at Bluidy. "And I'll just bet he knows where my uncle is, too!"

The rest of the children nodded their support. Dunleavey blinked his buggy eyes. He looked between the children and Bluidy and back again. Then, suddenly, he broke out in raucous, side-splitting laughter. Bluidy couldn't help but join him.

The children stood slack-jawed as tears streamed down Dunleavey's face. Quite obviously, their accusation was not being taken seriously. Dunleavey held his sides, trying to forestall the cramps that came with the contraction of each loud bray. He wiped the moisture from his eyes as the laughter began to subside.

"Such imaginations! You lot certainly have a knack for trying to start trouble! Imagine! An upstanding citizen like Mr. Bluidy – a thief?" He threatened to break into a new wave of laughter, but he suppressed the urge.

"Perhaps a few hours of pushing a mop around will teach you a little respect."

"But he's got a piece of the gold!" Smout grabbed the arm of Dunleavey's jacket, pointing toward Bluidy. "There! In his pocket!"

"Really?" Dunleavey's thin eyebrow shot up in curiosity. For a moment, the children quivered with the hope that Dunleavey believed them.

After what felt like an interminable silence, Dunleavey calmly plucked Smout's hand from his sleeve.

"I understand you are upset with the loss of your uncle, Mr. McManus. But, I'll thank you not to embarrass the Academy and hold your impertinent tongue." Dunleavey clipped each word.

Smout withered despondently. He took the

reprimand stoically though it rankled his stomach like a spoonful of castor oil. They were shuttled out to Bluidy's limousine and piled in for the trip to Port Edgar in South Queensferry.

So now, here he sat, brooding, trapped in the same car with the man whom he was certain had kidnapped his uncle and meant to steal perhaps the greatest historical treasure of Scotland's past!

He felt powerless.

He shoved his hands into his pockets, rewarded with a startlingly painful paper cut.

"Ow!" he hissed. He quickly withdrew his hand.

Rory leaned in toward his ear. "What's wrong?"

Smout squeezed the offending wound, trying to staunch the smarting pain.

"Nothing," he replied. "Just a stupid paper cut."

As he held the cut to his lips, his eyes suddenly widened. He wasn't helpless at all! He shot a quick look toward Bluidy and Dunleavey who, for the moment, seemed embroiled in a conversation about the upcoming Tattoo. Then Smout reached into his pocket and pulled out the two pieces of map. This was a clever war of minds, and Smout's pride felt a sudden surge. Bluidy was after the treasure. But, certainly, Smout was the smarter man. If they could find it before he did, they could use it to bargain for Uncle Bernie.

He looked at the back of the second piece of map. Five lines. Seven notes. A wisp of music written by Stevenson. The next clue. All they had to do was figure out what it meant. But they had to do it before Bluidy discovered their secret. If he found the treasure before they did, Uncle Bernie was as good as dead.

"The boy is in danger?" Gordon Staid felt the first urges of a violent sneezing attack festering in his nasal passages.

Detective Inspector Markham and Detective Sergeant MacGregor had arrived moments before and demanded an immediate audience with the school administrator.

Markham sat across from the rector in a standard office-type chair and nodded. MacGregor squirmed in a high-backed replica of a Holyrood Palace chair, trying to find a comfortable position. Somehow, the rigid chair brought childhood memories of visits with his school's headmaster flooding back. He eventually abandoned the enterprise and chose a standing position behind Markham who gave him a quizzical knot of hairy eyebrows in response. Markham shook his unkempt head and turned back to the rector.

"Yes, Mr. Staid," Markham began. "We believe Dr. McManus may have forwarded something on to his nephew. Something that was related to the project in which he was currently involved. A project we believe to have gotten him in a spot of trouble. Whatever was in that parcel may be of vital importance to our investigation. Worst case scenario, it might actually place the boy in mortal peril."

Staid felt his bulbous nose twitch. His school was populated with students who were sons and daughters of some of the United Kingdom's most important people! If anything he had done, or failed to do, had placed even a one of them in danger...no, he corrected. Not danger. Mortal peril! His nose erupted. The force of his sneeze caused Markham and MacGregor to both recoil in shock. Markham calmly wiped his lapel and pressed on.

"Has he received anything here at the school addressed from his uncle?" Markham paused, planting a wide palm on the rector's desk and scattering the neatly aligned pencils. "Anything you can remember might be of assistance."

Staid winced with anticipation of another violent attack of nasal explosions, but gratefully, the urge passed. Of course, he remembered the package recently arrived for young Master McManus. That bobble-headed scarecrow, Dunleavey, had brought in into his office. It was just before Bluidy's visit. The rector shuddered. At the time, he'd thought nothing of it.

"I had Mr. Bruce, one of our fourth years, deliver it to him. I had no idea it contained anything untoward," he assured the policemen. "Edinburgh Academy's first priority is to the safety of its students!"

Safe was, of course, the last place Smout and his odd little troupe currently found themselves.

He'd almost tipped his hand when the boy mentioned the gold, but years of careful pretending to be something he was not allowed him to retain his composure.

The boy kept fiddling with something in the pocket of his trousers. His thoughts raced. Perhaps what he was seeking was hidden amidst wads of bubblegum, discarded candy wrappers, and the other random detritus that normally took up residence in the pocket of a young school boy. He breathed deeply, regulating the pulse of his heart. He could not take it from the boy here. It was too risky. He would wait. He would wait until the time was right.

Then? Then he would strike.

CHAPTER TWENTY

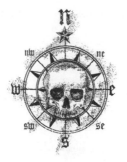

Shanghaied

Finn Fraser didn't expect much from life. Of course, he supposed it was only fair. After all, he didn't really put a whole lot into it. Some days, if he were able to build enough motivation, he would drag his hairy belly from the narrow twin bed and emerge from dingy grey sheets like a great, furry caterpillar from a cocoon. He would drop his feet, rough and coarse with thick yellow calluses, on the worn wooden floor. After a warm-up stretch and fifteen minutes of belly scratching, he would heft himself upright and shuffle to the loo.

Morning constitutional met, he'd pull on whatever shirt and pants he could find lying around the flat, don a pair of shoes, and drive his rusted-out gypsy cab to the docks where he'd try to pick up a few fares. Just enough wage to garner a bit of nosh and a round at the pub.

Today was not one of those days. The rest of Port Edgar greeted the day hours before, greeting their neighbors with hearty salutations and packing into cars or the early train. Finn, however, rattled the dirty panes on the single window of his bachelor's flat with his heavy snore. He had stayed up ridiculously late the evening prior watching some ridiculous suspense film on the telly. It was set in some quaint, seaside town. They wanted you to believe the villain was a pillar of the community and no one had any idea he was trapping people alive in coffins and setting them adrift on the open sea!

What it lacked in plot, though, it made up for with a bevy of beautiful girls, so he hadn't minded much. And the lack of sleep hadn't troubled him either. He could just stay in bed all day.

Nature, however, had its own plan for Finn.

The midday sun pressed insistently through an available crack in the window shade and prodded at Finn's closed eyelids. A guttural groan rumbled deep in his chest. He pulled the covers over his head, closing his eyes tighter against the sunshine that threatened to ruin his perfectly good day.

He was just about to slide back into unconscious oblivion when a seagull squawked a boisterous greeting outside the window. Finn jumped awake.

"What's a bloke got to do to get a bit of shuteye 'round here?" he barked. A collie from the place down the road yapped incessantly in reply.

"Caw!" Finn groaned. He lumbered to the cool box to grab a swallow of milk. The congealed lumps in the plastic jug, however, convinced him that perhaps venturing out into the sunshine might not be such an ill-conceived idea. He didn't remember today was the start of the Tattoo. Then again, he hadn't remembered to do the wash in a week either.

At half-past the hour, Finn closed and locked the front door behind him. Not that he had anything worth stealing, mind you. It was simply a matter of course. He stuffed his smelly frame into the pitted Ford Escort that served as the Fraser Transportation Fleet. He lowered the manual windows to activate the "natural oxygen ventilation system" advertised in clumsy hand-lettering on the driver's side door, then ratcheted the engine into a spluttering black cloud of reluctant smoke, and chugged off toward the port.

Just as he was about to pull onto the main road, a solitary lorry tore past, horn pealing, and skidded to a clumsy halt a few metres away. Finn pulled his car up short, his body weight hurling him forward, and tattooed his forehead smartly on the cracked leather dash. After the initial shock, Finn looked up angrily ready to hurl a string of curses. But any harsh words lodged in his throat as he caught a glimpse of the driver in the side glass. The giant of a man behind the wheel stared back at him stonily. The blood in Finn's veins chilled. For a moment, he feared he may actually have to run.

Suddenly, the stone-faced driver ground his vehicle into gear, throwing up clouds of road debris through Finn's open window. Finn rubbed the grit from his eyes and looked after the vehicle, its cargo bouncing madly about the open bed. He couldn't be sure if it was the dirt in his eyes, or leftover nightmares from last night's film, but Finn swore the truck carried five coffins.

Have you ever had the feeling you were headed in the wrong direction? As the limousine headed for Port Edgar Marina nestled on the southern shore of the Firth of Forth, Smout entertained that very feeling. He watched as a caravan of vehicles headed north across the Forth Bridge, the suspension span that connected Central Edinburgh with South Queensferry. He searched far ahead and behind their luxury car, but they appeared to be the only vehicle heading out of Scotland's capital. It seemed everyone was heading into Edinburgh for the opening ceremonies. Tonight thousands would gather on the Castle Esplanade to hear the rousing fanfare and witness the melodic precision of the Royal Scottish Dragoon Guard along with a brilliant programme of entertainment from hundreds of other international groups.

Smout sighed. It had always been a tradition that he and Uncle Bernie attended the opening festivities together. A lorry carrying a noxious cargo of cow manure rumbled past. Smout wished fervently he could be on it, stink and all. He wanted to be back in the city, back on the doorstep of their little flat, back in the midst of Uncle Bernie's organized chaos and Miss Dumbarton's interminable cribbage sessions and questionable culinary skills. His earlier resolve crumbled the further they got from the city. Who was he fooling? He wasn't cut out for all this adventure business. The thought suddenly occurred to Smout that he may never see his uncle again.

He shook his head. He couldn't let that happen. They would find the gold and his uncle. They just had to figure out how to get away from Bluidy and the exasperating Dunleavey. He stared out the window, searching for inspiration.

The Forth Bridge swooped in graceful peaks and valleys. It pointed toward a sky filled with clumps of fluffy cumulus clouds. When the limousine reached the southern end of the bridge, it turned to the West and headed into port.

The marina felt strangely deserted. A stray cat, probably in search of a scrap of fish, was the only sign of life they could see. They drove past a collection of corrugated metal sheds and modular buildings that comprised the businesses immediately servicing the marina. There was a blacksmith and forgemaster's shop for metal works, a chandler who dealt in sails and other supplies, and a repair shop, but everything appeared closed up tight.

The port's yacht club seemed to be the only place open for business. A few cars loitered in the lot. The two-toned brown wood and brick building offered cozy wrought-iron café seating on the red brick patio for those members who fancied a bit of fresh air. Eerily, however, the chairs were vacant, no members to be seen anywhere.

Smout shuddered. A perfect place for an ambush, he thought.

His eyes searched for a path of escape. His gaze fell upon a large, white sign that promised visitors hours of water fun with outboards, jet skis, and inboards, though he hadn't the foggiest notion what an inboard might be. A fat red arrow pointed toward the docks. Smout hoped it wasn't pointing straight toward their pending doom.

The limousine's wheels ground to a halt at the base of the long, wooden pier that stretched out far into the water. Mr. Grey had not been their driver for the ride from Edinburgh. Smout wondered where the big man had got off to. Dunleavey shuffled the children out into the crisp, breezy air. They bobbled together like the various boats tied off at their moorings.

Bogey pointed toward the five identical boxes lined up at the pier's edge. "Is it just me, or do those look a bit like coffins?"

"Don't be silly. You're just imagining things," Emma lied. She forced a smile, and swallowed hard. In fact, they looked exactly like coffins.

"It's a pity Mr. Grey couldn't join us," Dunleavey began as he stepped from the car and stretched his spindly legs. "He's missing a positively beautiful day."

Bluidy gave the five boxes a quick inventory, nodding his approval then took a place next to Dunleavey. He smoothed the travel wrinkles in his Harrods suit. "Oh, he'll be joining us soon enough. There were some last minute supplies needed for the ship. I expect he'll already be on board waiting."

"Waiting for what?" Bogey whispered into Mad Dog's ear. "A chance to make us walk the plank?"

Mad Dog managed a weak chuckle, but the thought was a bit sobering. Smout saw the nervous look on Emma's face. He puffed out his chest.

"Don't worry," he assured. "Doesn't matter if Dunleavey believed us or not. Bluidy won't try anything as long as he's around."

Just as they started to feel a bit more at ease,

Dunleavey sucked the wind from their sails.

"Well, now that we're here, I think I'll take my leave," Dunleavey stated. "I'm afraid boats make me a bit peaky. I think I'll try for a bit of refreshment at the Yacht Club."

The children erupted in an immediate chorus of disagreements. Dunleavey motioned for silence.

"Stop that nonsense at once. You'll be perfectly fine. I'm a stone's throw away at best. Now, I'm leaving you in Mr. Bluidy's charge."

"You can't do that!" Smout protested. He cast a worried look toward Bluidy who stood at the edge of the pier conversing in hushed undertones with his driver. The sharp-featured young man kept looking back their way.

Smout's voice dropped to a whisper. "It's not safe!"

"Don't be ridiculous! The ship isn't even leaving the dock. See? Tied up tight."

He gestured down the pier, toward the far end. The children turned as a collective unit to see two great masts towering into the sky. Smout counted nine different sails from bow to stern. Trim lines secured the great vessel, tethering her from the cleats to the dock, but the black oak of the ship's hull glowed in the light of the bright afternoon, a dark lady to woo the willing sailor.

Smout and his friends were as far from willing as one could possibly get. All the same, Dunleavey plopped a brilliant orange life-vest over Smout's head.

"But, as always, safety first! Wouldn't want any of you to come to harm, now would we?"

The now-familiar thump and drag of Bluidy's gait echoed behind them.

"Absolutely not," Bluidy agreed. "Well, my scrappy young crew, welcome to the *Hispaniola.*"

CHAPTER TWENTY-ONE

Black Jack

Inspector Markham felt his blood pressure rising by the second. The vein in his temple throbbed with the intensity of "Scotland the Brave". He and MacGregor were trapped at a standstill on Hanover Street, caught between a stalled lorry stocked with wildly squawking chickens and an awkwardly angled economy rental, insistently pressing forward on the right side of the road. Americans, no doubt. Why the neighbors from across the pond could not grasp the driving concept on this continent simply boggled the

Inspector's mind. Then again, the colonists always seemed to do things the hard way.

He leaned on the horn and it blatted a cranky note in the key of F. According to the rector at the Academy, the children were on a school trip, chaperoned by his secretary, out near South Queensferry. Meanwhile, he and MacGregor were slogging their way through the traffic in an effort to intercept young Master McManus and any information he might unwittingly be harboring regarding his uncle's recent disappearance.

A sudden flurry of white feathers snowed down on the window glass of the Inspector's car.

"I could fancy a bit of chicken right now," MacGregor murmured. Markham rewarded the interjection with a disparaging scowl. MacGregor shifted uncomfortably in the passenger seat.

"Well, it was only a thought," he simpered.

Markham scowled again for emphasis then leaned again on the horn. The single blaring note pealed into the mid-afternoon air.

There was no way they were getting on that ship.

Smout's fevered brain raced for a solution. Dunleavey had abandoned them, leaving them with the larcenous Bluidy. The man was a thief! He'd admitted as much to the children in the parlor of the Stevenson House. Who knew what other nefarious deeds the evil-looking man was capable? Smout eyed the five suspicious crates near the pier. Bogey was right. They did look like coffins. Smout began to suspect that Bluidy knew they had the clues and already had a plan to steal them and dispose of the children.

Smout knew the mysterious clues in his pocket held the solution for rescuing his uncle. He was certain. But they couldn't solve the mystery pushing mops about the deck of some modern-day pirate's ship. Or worse! They had to get back to Edinburgh. It was a moral imperative.

They needed a diversion. Suddenly, a light bulb went off in his head. He would resort to oldest stalling tactic known to childhood.

"I have to go to the loo," Smout announced.

"There's a head aboard the ship," Bluidy snapped grouchily. Smout craned his neck for a long, exaggerated look down the pier. The others caught his eye and nodded their agreement.

"I have to go, too," Bogey agreed picking up on Smout's ruse. He bounced back and forth in an awkward little dance.

"There's enough room for all of you to go!" Bluidy snapped. Emma seized her opportunity to add the coup de grace.

"But, Mr. Bluidy! I have to go, too, and I'm a girl! You can't possibly expect me to share facilities with a rowdy," she began.

"Mannerless," she wrinkled her nose in revulsion. Then she went in for the kill.

"Disgusting group of boys!" She clutched at her stomach in a dramatic display of repugnance. She collapsed in a violent fit of retching before stopping quite abruptly, affixing a stray lock of hair, and clearing her throat.

"Besides, it simply wouldn't be proper," she

concluded and nodded to her supporting cast. The boys crossed their legs, hovering breathlessly in anticipation.

Bluidy shook his head in submission.

"Oh, all right! There are facilities in that building there!" He pointed, irritated, at a small structure nearby.

"But, be quick about it. There's work to be done!" he snapped and stomped off toward the boat.

"That was fantastic!" Smout whispered excitedly. Emma smiled.

"Dramatic lessons. Mother thought it might help me overcome my shyness."

Smout grinned his approval.

The children, of course, had no intention of going anywhere near Bluidy or the *Hispaniola*. As soon as he was a comfortable distance down the pier, the children turned tail...and ran.

He'd fully expected it to happen. Timing had not been on his side since this whole mess had begun. But he was not discouraged. All that meant was he had to be creative and open to improvisation. Think on his feet. His brain raced, calculating the variables. As he watched the children run, he knew exactly what to do.

Smout and the rest of the children ducked behind a bulkhead to catch their breath. They didn't have much time before Bluidy realized they were not following him down the length of pier.

"So, what's the plan?" Mad Dog huffed between raspy gasps of breath.

"We take the rail back to Edinburgh. Solve Uncle Bernie's clues. We find the treasure then bargain with Bluidy to give up my uncle's location."

"That's brilliant," Bogey scoffed. "But how do you propose we get to the train station? We don't even know where it is!"

At that very moment, the entire Fraser Transportation Fleet skidded to a halt just to the left of the crouching group of children. Finn Fraser leaned out of the driver's window and scratched his three-day old stubble.

"I don't suppose you lot need a lift?"

The children exchanged surprised glances. Smout nodded wordlessly. Finn reached back and popped the rear door open.

"Hop on in then," he said and the group piled into the back seat. As Bogey closed the door behind them, Finn leaned back and eyeballed the curious troupe.

"You *are* going to pay me in something besides gumballs, right?" he asked.

Emma reached into her pocket and deposited a wad of bills into Finn's hand.

"Take us to the nearest train station," she demanded.

Finn grinned from ear to ear and tipped his hat. "Right away, Miss."

The boys stared in unabashed wonder as Emma passed the cash to Finn.

"I tutor on the weekends," she explained. Mad Dog let out a low whistle.

"I now have a decent reason to study," he mused. Emma just shook her head.

When they arrived at Dalmeny Station, they quickly booked five tickets all the way through to Waverley in Edinburgh.

"You'd best step lively, though," the woman at the ticket counter suggested. "Your train will be pulling out any minute."

If the woman thought it strange that five young people were travelling into the city unsupervised, she made no mention of it. Truth be told, she appeared to be glad of the distraction, the station being mostly deserted for the better part of the day. The only person that had been in since the early morning train was that strange-looking man that had come in just a few moments before the children. She wasn't sure where he'd got off to. She shrugged, bored again.

As soon as the children dashed off down the platform she popped her bright pink bubblegum and resumed thumbing through her gossip magazine to find out all about the latest celebrity nose job.

Halfway to the train, Smout pulled up short. Rory turned around to see what was wrong.

"What's the matter?" he asked.

"Now I really do have to go." The group sighed in unison. Smout grinned sheepishly.

"Well, hurry up or we'll miss the train," Rory urged.

Smout dashed to the men's room. He tried the first stall, but it was locked. He tried the second stall, but some less-thoughtful individual had left a foul present in the bowl.

"Caw, that's awful!" Smout wrinkled his nose in disgust. He danced to the last stall and pushed the door wide. He gasped in surprise as the skull-topped ebony cane raised high above his head and came crashing down.

Smout fainted clean away.

CHAPTER TWENTY-TWO

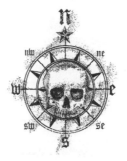

Sea Chantey

Clara Dumbarton didn't have noble aspirations. She didn't dream of marrying a royal and someday holding court in Buckingham Palace. She didn't fancy singing in front of millions on some silly television talent show and landing a recording contract. She was quite content with her lot, living in the simple guestroom of Mr. McManus' three-bedroom flat, watching her daytime stories, occasionally answering the bell for deliveries and the post, and picking up the clutter that seemed to accumulate on every flat surface in the house.

Well, occasionally picking up the clutter, anyway. At least when it suited her. Fortunately, Mr. McManus wasn't a very demanding employer, because it rarely suited her.

That's why she was fairly peeved when the bell rang, signaling the arrival of whatever unwanted visitor waited on the other side. She had invested most of her morning waiting to discover whether the beautiful blonde heiress, who was really the lost twin sister of the true heiress, who had been kidnapped by her half-brother, would choose her American oilman fiancé or the handsome Latin lover she had known in her youth. She couldn't possibly be bothered now!

She'd nearly not even heard the bell, or the insistent rapping at the door that almost immediately followed. She tended to raise the volume on the telly to stellar decibel levels. For a moment, she even considered further increasing the volume and ignoring the caller altogether, but propriety won out. She groaned as she hefted her creaky joints off the deliciously comfortable sofa. It was an advertisement break anyway. Oilman or Latin lover would wait till after a spot for Crispman's Crunchy Crisps.

As she clumsily weaved through stacks of books and piles of dirty laundry she promised to get to later, the knocking on the door became louder and more demanding. She stubbed her toe on one of Smout's toys.

"Ow! For the love of," she muttered, comically hopping like a drunken sailor as she grabbed her left toe. "Hold on! I'll be there in a spot!"

She picked up the offending toy, a truck that claimed to transform into some superhero robot, and set it on a nearby side table. Her dimples deepened as she thought of the young boy.

Poor little lamb. Every now and again, she was moved by some faint stirrings of pity and she'd pop a black bun in the oven for the boy. The pungent citrusy aroma of the finely-chopped peel and sweet, chewy currants with bits of almond always brought a toothy grin to the child's face. Her own mum used to comfort her with the very same recipe.

She had to admit, she was quite delighted that he'd had some young friends over the night before. The boy needed friends. Mr. McManus had said as much to her over a bottle of Glen Livet some weeks ago. Miss Dumbarton herself wasn't particularly given to drink, but with the damp chill of the Edinburgh evenings, she saw no harm in the occasional hot toddy. She seemed to recall that particular evening being especially chilly.

The odd assortment of children had seemed particularly interested in Mr. McManus' old chest. Honestly she hadn't thought about the dusty old thing in months, buried as it was under a hodgepodge of bric-a-brac. It seemed that cleaning hadn't suited her in quite a while. She'd left them to their own designs, secretly hoping that their endeavors would leave one less surface to clear away. She wasn't quite sure she liked the look of that young fellow, Maddagh, though. He looked a bit like a bulldog she'd known in her youth. Drooly old thing, it was. And prone to nipping at your heels. She shrugged. Nothing a good swat across the nose wouldn't cure. At any rate, they all seemed to be getting along, so she had let them be. What possible trouble could they get into?

He didn't remember screaming. He must have though because Rory, Mad Dog, Bogey and Emma came bursting into the men's lavatory shortly thereafter. When Emma spied some suspicious drops of blood on the tiled floor, she fussed and clucked over Smout like a mother hen, but could find no injury that might have caused the elongated ruby-red splatters leading out the rear exit of the washroom. Rory and Mad Dog helped Smout to a sitting position.

"What happened?" Bogey asked, worry furrowing his pale forehead.

Bluidy's name was the only coherent word Smout managed to form as he grabbed Rory's arm for support.

"Bluidy?" Mad Dog exclaimed. He growled. "Where is he? I'll give him a proper thrashing."

Rory's eyes followed the blood trail toward the exit. "I don't think that's the best idea, Mad Dog.

191

It doesn't look like Smout got hurt, but somebody lost some blood here. We'd better get out of here, or we could be next."

Mad Dog slapped Smout on the back as the small boy stood. "Maybe our boy here got a swipe in. Cracked that twisty scar face a good one in the nose, huh?"

Smout shook his head. "I can't remember."

"Well, come on, you lot. The train's about to leave. We can figure it out once we're safely on our way back to the city."

Now, Smout sat slumped against the window of the two o'clock into Waverly, waiting for the rhythmic clack-clack of the rails to put enough distance between him and Bluidy. He was certain Bluidy had meant to crush his head with the cane.

Smout's eyes roved over his friends. In spite of the danger they seemed to be facing, they all seemed strangely peaceful. Mad Dog snored with a deep, resounding vibrato. Smout stifled a snigger. He would not be happy when he awoke. A large, wet patch of drool spread across the sleeve of his shirt where Bogey's face smashed awkwardly against him. Rory gazed serenely out the window as the green patchwork blur of countryside zoomed past.

A melodic humming floated in counterpoint over the clack of the train wheels. It played out, modulated into another key then repeated. It reminded Smout of the old sea chanteys, the working songs pirates would chant to coordinate line heaving and other deck work. He looked over at Emma. She had the second scrap of map resting on her lap. Her head was tilted back, leaning on the wall of their compartment. The index finger of her right hand weaved a smart little pattern in the air, conducting her little impromptu concert. Smout leaned forward.

"Have you figured it out yet?" he asked. Emma turned her head.

"I'm not sure. I think I've basically got the melody, but I've no idea what it means. Are you absolutely certain this has something to do with Robert Louis Stevenson?" she asked.

"It must. The other clues have, and you heard Bluidy at Stevenson's house. Stevenson used to compose music for the flageolet. This has to be one of his pieces!"

"If you can believe the word of that lying crook," Rory muttered, joining the conversation.

"But why would he lie about something like that?" Emma asked.

"Seems to me like that bloke would lie to his own mother if it meant he could score an extra quid," Rory grumbled.

"Well, let's assume he didn't lie about the music and this is one of Stevenson's pieces. If the first clue led us to *Treasure Island*, and the second clue led us to *A Child's Garden of Verses*, where does this one lead us?" Emma asked.

Smout opened his mouth to reply then sank back dejectedly when he realized he absolutely no idea what his uncle may have been trying to tell him with the small snatch of music. Emma tapped the paper with her forefinger.

"The key is the key," she mumbled. "The key is the key. Smout, I have an idea. All of these notes have names, you know. Letter names."

"Yeah. So?" Rory said.

"What if the letter names of the notes spell out the next clue?" Emma responded.

Smout's eyes widened as he caught on to what Emma was suggesting. "Like the dominoes spelled out garden?"

Emma nodded vigorously. "Exactly!"

Mad Dog and Bogey roused from their nap, stirred by the excited voices.

"What's all this?" Mad Dog began then noticed the damp stain on his shirt. He wiped so vigorously at the offending mark the friction nearly started a fire. "Ugh!"

"We think we may have solved the next clue!" Smout jabbered like a field mouse on helium. "Go ahead, Emma. What's it say?"

"Okay. Well," she began. "To figure out what the names of the notes are, you have to look at the key signature."

Smout's eyes opened wide. "The key is the key!"

Emma nodded excitedly. "Yes. Depending

195

on the key, the notes could spell out an entirely different word because the notes would have different letter names. If we look at this piece, there are no sharps or flats in the key signature. Those are the little symbols that tell you to play the notes lower or higher. Since there aren't any, that means we are in the key of C. If that's right, then this first note is an A."

Rory nodded in excitement. "Go on."

"So, if this is an A, then this next one is C, then this one is an A again. Then someone scribbled this funny little lowercase 'R' here," she continued.

"Hold on," Mad Dog ordered. He moved to the window glass and breathed a heavy fog across its surface. As Emma called out each successive letter name, Mad Dog traced it with a fat finger onto the window before the condensation faded. When she called out the final letter, Mad Dog expelled a fresh cloud of breath across the figures he'd traced. Bogey wrinkled his nose and waved a hand back and forth in front of his face.

"Ugh! Morning breath! Nasty!" he said.

Mad Dog stuck out his tongue then read the letters.

"A-B-R-A-C-A-D," Mad Dog announced. He leaned back, looking at the letters from another angle as if the change of direction would change the letters. It didn't.

"Abracad?" Mad Dog questioned. "That doesn't make a bit of sense. I guess you were wrong." He frowned.

"We're getting nowhere." Smout sank back heavily into his seat.

"Nowhere but trouble," Bogey declared.

A gloomy despair settled over the group. Mad Dog and Bogey were right. They'd lost their chaperone. They were no closer to finding the missing treasure or Uncle Bernie, and for all they knew, Bluidy was hot on their heels. He'd already taken a vicious swing at Smout. Who knew what he would do if he caught up to them?

Suddenly, Emma jumped up. "I'm a complete idiot!"

"I'll second that!" Mad Dog cheered. Rory rewarded him with a quick slap to the back of his head.

"What?" Mad Dog retorted. "She said it first!"

He rubbed the back of his head. Emma pointed at the slip of paper. "Look! Do you see this phrase here? *D.C. al fine*? It means go back to the beginning and repeat until you come to the double bar line. The word's not finished! Goodness. Mother would throttle me after all that money she spent on piano lessons! Mad Dog! Quick! Add these letters. A-B-R-A! Ha! Read it now!"

Mad Dog scrawled the last letters. He sucked in a full lungful and breathed a last hot fog of air across the letters on the window. As if by magic, a complete word materialized on the glass.

Abracadabra.

CHAPTER TWENTY-THREE

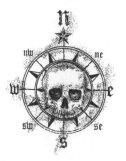

Golden Opportunity

Markham feared the worst. The knot growing in the pit of his stomach had started when he and MacGregor arrived in the nearly deserted Port Edgar and found no sign of the children, their chaperone, or the mysterious Mr. Bluidy.

"Are you certain you've got the proper location?" Markham questioned MacGregor. MacGregor dutifully flipped open his black book and consulted his notes.

"Spot on, sir. I never miss on the details."

Markham voiced a fairly guttural response. "Quite right. Quite right."

He stuffed his hands into his trouser pockets and surveyed the general area. "But then," he paused. "Where in the Queen's name are they?"

That had been over a half-hour ago. They questioned the scant few locals. A sketchy-looking cab driver they found sitting in front of the yacht club mentioned he had dropped a group of un-chaperoned children at the train station. The anxiety in Markham's gut grew exponentially. A rumbling belch bubbled up from his innards. Why would the children dash off, and especially without their chaperone? Young Smout and his friends were in serious trouble, his gut warned. He and MacGregor made for the station with haste.

Never had he wished more that his gut was mistaken than when they discovered a bloody handkerchief in the men's lavatory at Dalmeny Station and a blood trail leading out to the platform. The two policemen followed the trail of red right to where the drops stopped... at the tracks where the two o'clock into Waverly had pulled away not long before.

"Would you care for more tea?" Miss Dumbarton reached for the cozy and lifted it over her guest's china cup.

"*Si*, please," he answered in heavily accented, slightly strangled English. A stony lump of teacake was lodged in Arturo Sandoval's throat. He welcomed the rather weak Darjeeling the old woman offered him hoping fervently it would help wash the stale obstruction down his gullet.

He had expected a much different reception from the housekeeper when he had rapped so smartly on the door. Most people found his odd appearance off-putting at best, looking more like a clay-faced golem of Jewish folklore than a brilliant scientist. He was prepared to be greeted with nervous looks and hurried along with tales of a fictitious cake burning in the oven. For whatever reason, however, Clara Dumbarton appeared to have taken a shine to him and had invited him in almost immediately. He looked over the lace doily and smiled crookedly at the old woman. For a moment, he swore she was batting her lashes at him. He rubbed his droopy eyes. Maybe he was imagining things.

He certainly hadn't imagined the frantic call from his employer. The boy had escaped, almost definitely with the information necessary to finding the treasure. He had ordered Arturo to steal into the McManus home and search for anything that might point them in the direction of the boy or the treasure.

Arturo had decided to pose as one of McManus' colleagues from the museum. He leaned in toward Miss Dumbarton who welcomed the proximity of the odd little man.

"So, you can see," he continued. "It is of much importance that I see Mr. McManus' notes. They are vital to the project we are working on at the museum."

"Oh, yes. Of course!" Miss Dumbarton nodded and fluffed the bun in her hair.

"So, Mr. Sandoval, is it? That's Latin, right?"

Arturo nodded. He was rewarded with a wide, denture-filled smile. Miss Dumbarton winked. Arturo gulped audibly. Miss Dumbarton slowly removed her bifocals, letting them hang by their golden chain. She edged a bit closer to the dumpy little man.

Sandoval's right index finger began a rapid staccato on his right leg as Miss Dumbarton placed a liver-spotted hand on his left thigh. As the old woman leaned in, a peculiar bouquet of liniment and tuna wafted through his twitching nostrils. Miss Dumbarton tittered like a schoolgirl.

"I know a bit of Spanish myself, you know. For example, someone might describe a handsome gentleman like yourself as *muy caliente*." She gave Sandoval's thigh a proper squeeze.

In the next few moments, several events transpired in rapid succession. Sandoval squawked, or at least made a valiant attempt before the dry teacake fully obstructed his airway and he began to choke violently. Without the aid of her glasses, Miss Dumbarton fumbled over the tea tray and knocked a full cup of hot tea into Sandoval's lap. As the scalding beverage soaked through the thin fabric of his pants, he leapt to his feet. He wiped furiously at the pain, but only thing he succeeded in wiping out was Miss Dumbarton as she toppled to the floor.

"Oh, my goodness gracious!" she exclaimed. She rocked to and fro for a few moments, wobbling like an egg-shaped children's toy, then finally succeeded in righting herself. She fumbled for her bifocals, perching them on the end of her nose.

"Heavens!" she shouted as the hopping Spaniard came into focus. "I'm so terribly, terribly sorry. I'll fetch you a rag at once."

She immediately bustled off toward the kitchen. With all the hopping, Sandoval managed to loose the lump of cake. He greedily sucked in a few deep breaths, glad of the oxygen even if did still carry fishy reminisces of the old woman. He wiped his weepy eyes and watched her waddle off down the hall. He winced at the twinge of pain still lingering in his legs then shook it away. This was his golden opportunity to steal a few glances about the flat. He wasn't going to waste it dwelling on a little discomfort. With a bit of luck, he could find a clue to the boy's whereabouts and quickly escape the amorous affections of the old hag.

He looked around the parlor for a hint, a sign. His gaze landed on Bernard McManus' desk. The old pine roll-top had seen better days, nicked and scarred from any number of the historical battles Smout and his uncle had reenacted in the small room. He poked through a stack of papers. Nothing promising there. Just a bunch of stodgy, scholarly scribblings.

His droopy gaze wandered to the floor-to-ceiling bookshelves lining the north wall. He very nearly jumped from his own skin as he came face to face with the withered features of the shrunken head resting at eye level. He stared at the wizened raisin of a face. It sort of resembled the old woman, Sandoval thought. Perhaps she was a witch and had cast an evil spell on some other poor, unfortunate soul that had joined her for tea. He swallowed hard, and rubbed his neck.

Remember what you came for, he thought. He looked around. Suddenly, he let loose a long, low whistle. Rows upon rows of tightly crammed shelves ran the full-length of the room. Books exploring every subject occupied every available square centimeter of space. Sandoval even found a copy of a robotics manual wedged between books on Mayan temples and the American Revolution. But the titles that really caught Sandoval's eye were neatly arranged on one of the lower shelves. A shelf that could easily be reached by a ten-year old boy. Those books stood out from the rest, each binding neatly aligned in a perfectly regimented row. Less dust had gathered here, suggesting a frequent reader visited these titles often. Sandoval trailed a finger over the intriguing titles.

Kidnapped.

The Strange Case of Dr. Jekyll and Mr. Hyde.

The Body Snatchers.

A boy's array of adventure titles, to be certain. And all of them penned by Robert Louis Stevenson. The Spaniard picked up the last title, turning the old leather-bound volume over in his hand. The gilt-lettering of the book's title sparkled, even in the somewhat dim light.

Treasure Island.

He opened the green leather cover, the slightly musty smell of old book drifting up from the brilliantly illustrated frontispiece. He read the flowing inscription on the facing title page which echoed a famous quote from one of Scotland's most favored sons.

"To my dearest Smout. No man is lonely without a friend. May this book be the first of many. Mother."

Sandoval felt a momentary lump rise in his throat and swallowed hard. He forced a strict cough, fearing the cake was making a return visit.

"Those are wee Smout's books. I've never seen a child so in love with books as that lad."

Miss Dumbarton's voice startled him. The book nearly dropped into the puddle of tea welling on the floor. For a moment, he bobbled it precariously then returned it to the shelf. Miss Dumbarton reached out, handing him a kitchen rag that rated somewhere about midway on the ladder of clean. He offered a weak smile and rubbed at the damp stain.

"Oh?" he managed weakly.

"Yes, if he wasn't curled up in that chair right there, nose buried in one his stories, he could be found, like as not, at that dusty old bookshop, searching for another."

Sandoval froze. This sounded promising. He turned up the wattage on his crooked smile and took her wrinkled hand in his own.

"Book shop? And what book shop might that be, my dearest *señorita*?"

Miss Dumbarton lowered her head coquettishly at Sandoval's freshened interest.

"That would be Gubbins Corner, of course. Down on Lawnmarket. Fergus Oxfam's the proprietor. Lovely man, of course. Tried to court me once, but I prefer my men a bit younger."

She smiled widely just as her dentures slipped out of place.

When they found the gold, Arturo Sandoval promised himself he would buy a beautiful villa on a perfect beach where the water was as blue as sapphires and he would surround himself with women.

All of them would have their original teeth.

CHAPTER TWENTY-FOUR

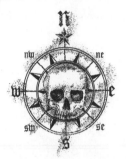

Turn Cat in the Pan

He'd almost gotten away with it. He'd nearly had the boy and his friends safely secured on the boat along with the five crates to hold the gold. But he'd let himself be fooled. Jack Bluidy was not the type of man to tolerate fools. He took a measured sip from the glass on the table before him, sighing heavily. He hadn't even had a chance to explain himself to Smout.

When he had first learned of Bernie's mysterious disappearance, Bluidy and his associate, Mr. Grey, paid a visit to Bernie's office at the museum, searching for answers. Bernie's university intern, a gabby young chap, to be sure, offered information to excess. Of course, it pertained mostly to the biology and habits of the large tarantula he held in his hands and precious little about Bernie. He had been so engrossed in his speech regarding the spider he had nearly been run down by the odd, pudgy Spaniard barreling from Bernie's cluttered office. Mr. Grey had given chase while Bluidy set the discombobulated intern to rights. When Mr. Grey had returned, he reported he had lost the Spaniard, but not before he had wrestled a heavy gold coin from the man's grasp. The Louis d'Or. Stolen, yes. But, from a thief. And one, Bluidy suspected to have some part in Bernie's disappearance.

Suddenly, Bluidy slammed his glass down with such force, crystalline shards exploded over the table surface. One piece flew up and caught Bluidy's cheek. He swatted it away and a bead of red instantly welled to the surface. Bluidy touched a finger to the spot. Blood. A wry smile tugged at the corner of his lips. A funny thing, blood. Almost five litres of it

211

coursed through the average adult body. It determined if you were descended from paupers or kings. It could prove beyond a shadow of a doubt whether the girl on the morning tram was your sister, or the lad who bagged your groceries at the local market was your brother - or whether the small, frail boy with the smattering of odd freckles was your son.

Bluidy didn't need a blood test to realize Smout was his boy. Granted, he hadn't seen the lad since he was a wee tike, playing at his mother's feet while the surf rolled into the Yellowcraigs shoreline. Victoria McManus' laugh had tinkled like a bell as she watched her boy play with the wild abandon reserved for the young. Her blue eyes had sparkled with pure delight.

That was how he knew. The moment he saw Smout's eyes, he knew. The boy had her eyes. Sapphire blue and twinkling with the hope of adventure.

Bluidy sighed as memories came flooding back – memories of long walks over the rolling dunes, a tiny hand, curled in his own. Of bubbling excitement as clumps of sand flew willy-nilly while the toddler dug for a buried shell. The shrill squeal of delight when the "treasure" was unearthed.

For a fleeting moment, Bluidy wondered how he could have ever left them – left them to seek the glory of fame and fortune elsewhere. He had kept tabs on them, of course. He wasn't a complete monster. He'd even arranged an anonymous monthly stipend through an Edinburgh solicitor to help provide for them. The discreet inquiry here and there kept him aware of the events in their lives. When he learned of Victoria's disappearance, he'd nearly abandoned his search for worldly treasures and rushed back to Edinburgh to his son's side. Nearly. A tug of regret pulled momentarily at his conscience.

Then, as quickly as that feeling of remorse arrived, the long, lonely memories of another young boy, abandoned and forgotten on the steps of his West Pilton home, cleaved through the guilt and slammed him squarely back into the present.

No one had come back for him.

Truth was, you could not count on family.

Blood might be thicker than water, but it could not buy security. Gold could.

He shook himself. Waxing melancholy would not serve his purpose. He needed to remember what was important. He had to find the treasure!

He knew it had been risky answering Bernie's letter. He admitted he had been greatly surprised when he received – no, he corrected himself – when *Bluidy* received his older brother's correspondence. Duncan McManus no longer existed. His brother hadn't any clue to whom he had truly written. He merely assumed he was writing to a wealthy patron of improbable archaeological enterprises. The sheer folly of the venture had precluded him from seeking capital from regular channels. Indeed, Bernie's claim was nearly too fantastic to believe. But Bernie was adamant in his assertion that he had found lost correspondence – a tattered letter written by Robert Louis Stevenson to his good friend, W.E. Henley – that claimed Stevenson had discovered the lost treasure of Bonnie Prince Charlie – and moved it. Moved it and sketched out a map of its new location for Lloyd Osborne, son of his new wife, Fanny Osborne.

Stevenson's original map had been "lost" and the author had been required to draw another when *Treasure Island* went to press. But suppose Stevenson had actually hidden the original map for Osborne, perhaps in some family heirloom? What if he left a trail of clues hidden between the pages of his work that would lead young Osborne to the hidden prize? Indeed, Stevenson himself often mused: "For my part, I travel not to go anywhere, but to go. I travel for travel's sake. The great affair is to move."

Bernie firmly held that the author scrawled out the initial map of *Treasure Island* in that long ago cabin in Braemar to entice the lad to get out and experience the life sometimes denied Stevenson due to his poor health.

It was an intriguing puzzle, delicious as mysteries went.

But to accept Bernie's proposal meant risking recognition. And, of course, that he could come face to face with his son. The past Bluidy had tried so hard to leave behind lurked in the shadows, ready to pounce.

True, he had not seen his elder sibling for many years. Surely, though, he didn't suppose that the mere change of his name, Duncan McManus to Jack Bluidy, would serve as a convincing disguise to his elder brother. But Bluidy felt confident that his outward appearance, with his sun-leathered skin and winding scar, had morphed his countenance so that his sibling would feel not a twinge of recognition. The rough, limping rogue bore little resemblance to the fair, round-cheeked young man he had once been. Besides, the siren call of the gold was too great. So, he had risked discovery to take part in this grand adventure. But he was not the only one pursuing the treasure. Bluidy had not given much credence to the Spaniard as a serious threat. It had not occurred to him the sloppy man was working for someone else. He had been quite taken aback when he saw the spindly, little secretary attacking his son in Dalmeny Station. Never judge a book by its cover, Bluidy realized. Fortunately, Bluidy had succeeded in giving him a proper crack on the head and gave his son the chance he needed to escape. Bluidy had given chase, but Dunleavey had eluded him.

Now, he thought as he held his face in his hands, his brother was missing, he was no closer to finding the treasure, and his son was lost on the streets of Edinburgh with a potential killer close on his heels.

Waverley Station garnered its name from the novels of the same name written, of course, by the great Sir Walter Scott. The station was a busy beehive nestled in the steep, narrow valley between the two faces of Edinburgh, Old Town and New Town, in the hollow once occupied by the Nor Loch. In the late 18th and early 19th centuries, Nor Loch was a festering sewer of waste, home to more than a few dead bodies.

As Smout spied the familiar clock tower high atop the Balmoral Hotel, he found himself fervently wishing his current quest would not end so dismally. The clock's erect hands saluted high noon as the

Dalmeny train pulled into Waverley Station. Smout checked the broad face of his multi-purpose wristwatch. It lagged two minutes behind. His spindly fingers reached to adjust the slower timepiece when he recalled the Balmoral clock keepers purposely kept the clock two minutes fast, a valiant effort to keep travelers on time for their trains. He smiled wryly. If it were only that easy, he thought.

Smout bounded to his feet. "Come on, you lot! The clock's ticking, and Uncle Bernie's counting on us!"

The motley crew rubbed errant sleep from their eyes, grabbed the odd satchel, and bounded from their compartment heading for the platform. Smout's looked up at the intricate network of glass and beams on the station's ceiling. It occurred to him they looked like the veins and sinews of some great beast. The echo of Uncle Bernie's voice complained grouchily from somewhere in Smout's memory.

"It's a regular beast trying to find a train on time, here!"

Smout smiled at the memory. No. Trains in

and out of Waverley didn't always arrive or depart on time, but the large boards posted in the station did their best to inform expectant travelers.

"Do you suppose we might grab a bite before we dash off?" Bogey rubbed his growling belly. "I'm positively starving."

Rory shook his head. "No time. We don't know how close Bluidy is behind us. What we need is a safe place to hide while we figure out the next clue."

"What I *need* is a flame-broiled burger with cheese," Bogey grumbled.

"No," Smout began. "Rory's right. We need a hideout, and I think I have the perfect place. Come on. Let's get out of here before Bluidy shows up and spots us."

They had been spotted, alright, but not by Bluidy. Dunleavey tried to lean casually against a cash point machine, hiding behind the fold of the afternoon paper.

He had almost lost them after Bluidy surprised him at Dalmeny Station. As he thought about it, he was positively flummoxed at how Bluidy had arrived there so quickly and foiled his attempt to grab the boy. He winced as pain seared over his right eye like a white hot poker. He searched his pockets for a handkerchief. Funny. He thought he'd had two. He shrugged and dabbed gingerly at the two-inch gash Bluidy's cane had viciously opened there. He had to admit, for a man with a pronounced limp, Bluidy was decidedly agile. Dunleavey had only narrowly escaped, leaping onto the departing train as it chugged toward Edinburgh. Bluidy was onto his game now, but no matter. The old pirate was chasing the gold as well. He wouldn't dare rat him out for fear of giving himself away.

The children were very nearly on top of him before he realized he had left himself visible. He quickly flipped the news open to hide his face. He tried to look casual as the group passed. One of the children brushed against the paper, grousing loudly about being hungry, but moved on toward the Market Street exit, unawares.

As soon as they were out of earshot, he

allowed himself a long exhale of relief. He was about to toss the paper aside when an older man, stubble glittering on his wrinkled cheek, shuffled near.

"Oi! You done with that?"

The old man, looking strangely crooked with his buttons fastened in the wrong holes, pointed to the paper. Dunleavey nearly scowled at the old beggar, nose wrinkling instinctively at the dirty, stained coat and wellies strangely out of place in the fair weather. The encroaching appearance of a pair of transport police gave him an idea. He began to shrug off his own tailored coat.

"I'll do you one better. How about a trade?"

The old man flashed a nearly toothless grin at the proposition and immediately began to shed his coat. Dunleavey nearly gagged at the odor wafting up as the old man handed it off to him, but he stifled the reflex. He was betting that Bluidy hadn't alerted the police to his description after the attack at Dalmeny, but there was no sense in taking chances. If the police were after him, they'd be searching for a crisply-suited secretary, not a tatty vagrant in a stained coat.

Satisfied with his impromptu disguise, he gave a curt nod to the old man and started to sprint across the terminal. As he neared the patrolling policemen, however, he caught himself. Play the part, he thought.

He slowed down, put a hitch in his step, and shuffled slowly toward the exit stairs. He was nearly there when a gruff, official voice suddenly called out across the way.

"Hey, there! Yeah. You in the coat."

Dunleavey cringed. He responded, lowering his voice so it sounded like years of whisky and cigars had leavened their damage.

"Yeah?"

The policeman cocked his head. He seemed to sense that something was a bit hinky. Dunleavey began to sweat inside the dirty coat. The policeman satisfied himself with delivering his rehearsed warning.

"Be on your way, then. Don't want your kind bothering the working folk 'round here. Oh, pardon

222

me, sir."

The policeman accidentally bumped into the beggar, now sporting his smart tailored jacket. The old man puffed at the courtesy. He straightened his shoulders and nodded, walking proudly away.

Dunleavey lowered his gaze, shielding his features from the police.

"Just on my way, sir. Thank you, sir."

The policeman, satisfied he had done his job, departed to roust a youth playing guitar on the other side of the station. Dunleavey breathed a sigh of relief. He was safe for now.

With that, he shuffled up the exit stairs. As he reached the top, he quickly looked in both directions, hoping to catch a glimpse of the children. His vision swam with gaggles of t-shirt clad tourists, businessmen with leather attachés, and laughing groups of knap-sacked university students. The trill of his phone jingled in his pocket. He reached for it, hoping no one found it odd that a homeless vagrant owned a cellular device.

"What?" he quipped into the receiver. An

excited voice jabbered on the other end of the line. A wide smile broke out across Dunleavey's face.

"Gubbins Corner? I'm on my way."

He snapped the mobile closed and jogged off into the clear, bright August afternoon.

CHAPTER TWENTY-FIVE

The Smoking Lamp

"Gubbins? What's a gubbins?"

Mad Dog scratched his head as the assorted group barreled into Fergus Oxfam's bookshop.

The bell on the door tinkled wildly, rousing the sleepy proprietor from his nap. The fire in the hearth had burned down to glowing embers hours ago, but the fever burning in the eyes of the five young children piling into his shop burned brighter than any flame log and coal could muster.

"Mr. Oxfam! Mr. Oxfam!"

"What? Oh! My goodness! What's all the fuss?" Oxfam muddled about, searching for his glasses. He perched them on the thin bridge of his nose and squinted through the out-dated prescription. His bushy eyebrows popped up in recognition.

"Smout, my dear boy! How are you? Off on holiday, are we?"

"Yes, sir." Smout winced at the lie, but the less Mr. Oxfam knew, the safer he would be.

"That's a bit of luck. Such a beautiful day to be out and about. Usually so dismal this time of year. You know, I was wondering when I was going to see you again. And you brought some friends?"

Oxfam's observation gave Smout momentary pause. He hadn't really thought about it. Other than his books, he'd never really had friends. Smout looked around at the four companions who had joined him on his quest. Yes, he thought. He supposed he might just be able to call them friends.

"Yes, Mr. Oxfam. My friends and I," he paused, savoring the foreign taste of the word – friends. "Well, we're looking for something."

"Of course, lad! I've got it right here!" Oxfam rocked himself out of his wing-back chair and shuffled behind the counter.

Smout and his friends looked round at each other. Was it possible Mr. Oxfam had the gold? Had Uncle Bernie given it to the elfin bookshop owner for safekeeping?

"That's impossible!" Mad Dog gave voice to what they all were thinking. They turned as a unit to watch Mr. Oxfam shuffle back toward them carrying a small package wrapped in twine.

"Here it is. Came in just yesterday." He handed the package to Smout. It bore a remarkable resemblance to the package Uncle Bernie had forwarded to the Academy. Secured in brown paper, the parcel was twenty centimeters long by thirteen centimeters across. Its depth bordered on two centimeters.

"No way that's £5m in gold," Rory whispered.

"£5m in gold?" Fergus Oxfam guffawed. His sight may have been sketchy, but there was nothing wrong with the old man's hearing.

227

"Five pounds, maybe. Least that's what the book in that package is worth, give or take." He blinked like an owl at the blank faces before him. Oxfam took a few more shuffling steps toward them.

"It's the book you ordered last week, Smout. Remember?"

Smout took a few moments to dig past the memories of the recent wild events. He could not remember placing an order with the shopkeeper.

"I didn't order any books, Mr. Oxfam."

"You didn't? Hm. I was quite certain." He scratched his bald head, puzzled. "Oh, now I remember. Your uncle came in, this Friday past, and asked me to hold it for you."

"My uncle?"

Oxfam nodded. "Aye. Said you might find it interesting reading."

"Maybe your uncle left another clue," Emma spoke in hushed tones.

"Say, would you nippers care for some tea? I think I've got a few shortbread rounds in the back," Oxfam offered.

"I'll say!" Bogey agreed heartily. "I'm starved."

"I'll just go off and fetch them then." He started to wander toward the back of the shop.

"Mr. Oxfam?" Smout called. The old man turned with the speed of molasses.

"Yes, boy?"

"Do you suppose you might have a spot where we could meet for a bit? Someplace quiet and out of the way?" They could not take the chance that the old man's keen ears might pick up any more details of their scheme.

"There's that little table, of course. Down the stairs. Back among the stacks. Keep an eye out for Flint, though. I'm not sure where he's got off to. Hunting for mice, I suppose. Just as long as he doesn't knock the guard into the fire again. Goodness! Can you imagine? With all these books in here, one small ember could turn this place into an inferno! Maybe I'll just open a tin of kippers for him. That should settle him. Here, Flint. Here, kitty, kitty."

The knot of children waited, Oxfam's mumbling voice growing fainter as he retreated into the recesses of the shop. Smout clutched the package and darted off through the maze of bookshelves.

"Come on!"

He led them past countless titles and down the stairs to a round, wooden table nestled in a secluded corner. A small window at street level, paned in pebbled glass, allowed a few diffuse rays of light to spill onto the table. Curious spiders trailed down from webs. They didn't see many visitors. Mad Dog blew a curling cloud of dust from the table. Smout's resultant sneeze sent a flurry of wet snot across the table to shower Bogey.

"Awk!"

Smout's eyes widened behind his glasses. He was not used to this friends thing at all. "Sorry about that. Allergies."

Bogey waved him off. "No worries. Remind me to show you my mural some time."

"What's that?"

"Um, nevermind. What's in the package?"

As the others pulled up rickety stools round the small table, Smout tore into the wrapping with gusto. Brown ribbons of paper fluttered to the ground, forming a haphazard litter pile. Smout held up the package contents. Puzzlement gave way to disappointment as frown lines furrowed their faces.

They had all expected to find another mysterious clue. Something that would put them back on the trail of Charlie's gold. Instead, what Smout held aloft in his pale little hand was a rather pedestrian, boringly rectangular, book. Normally, Smout would have been quite excited, but compared to his recent adventures, the regimented typeface sat dully on the page.

"*The Wrong Box*?" Rory read the book's title.

Mad Dog snatched the tome from Smout's hands. "What's that supposed to mean? Is that some sort of joke?" He riffed quickly through the pages, but found nothing out of the ordinary.

"There's not even any pictures." He carelessly let the book fall onto the floor where it landed half-open, pitched like a tent. Smout picked up the book and wedged it into his trouser pocket.

"I suppose Uncle Bernie just expected I'd like to read it."

"Well, it's no matter now. Let's have a look at that last clue before Bluidy comes calling."

As Smout fished the crumpled piece of map from his pocket, the bell on the front door jingled, echoing faintly into their little recess. Slow, deliberate footsteps overheard dislodged little plumes of dirt from the seams in the floorboards. Grit rained down in dirty clouds on their heads. Suddenly, they heard voices. Each of the children held a breath. If it was Bluidy, they had nowhere to run.

They strained to hear the dull conversation as it drifted down to their hidden corner, but to no avail. A heavy thunk sounded from the floor above. Their hearts hammered rapidly. After a few moments, they heard the shrill ring of the cash register. Everyone sighed in relief. Just a customer.

Relieved, they turned back to the clue. Rory pointed at the scrap.

"Ok. Well, everyone knows abracadabra is a

magical word. Think, Smout. Do any of Stevenson's stories have anything to do with magic?"

Smout shook his head. Emma's nose twitched. "The Wizard of West Bow."

"No, Emma. Stevenson didn't write a story called that. I'm fairly certain," Smout asserted.

"No, silly. It's not a story." She leaned in, dropping her voice to a whisper. "A lot of people think Stevenson based Dr. Jekyll on the infamous Deacon Brodie."

Mad Dog grinned in a sudden burst of inspiration. "The chap the pub's named after?"

Emma rolled her eyes. "Yes, the chap the pub's named after. But, what he's really known for is being an upright member of society who turned bad. He was a well-known Mason and cabinet maker by day, but a thief by night."

"I think the Stevenson family owned a wardrobe made by Brodie," Smout offered. Emma nodded.

"But some historians believe Stevenson actually based Jekyll on another upstanding citizen who turned out to be a very nasty character – Major Thomas Weir – the <u>Wizard</u> of West Bow."

Arturo Sandoval frowned. He thumbed through the few scant bills he'd just managed to collect from the register. A few pounds, at best. He wondered how the bookshop even managed to stay in business.

"What a waste," he grumbled as they walked up the High Street.

"Stop grousing. I don't know why you felt the need to rob the place, anyway," Dunleavey snapped. He gestured emphatically to the pound notes in Sandoval's beefy grip. "When we find the treasure, that chicken scratch will be an insignificant drop in the bucket."

Sandoval raised his arms in protest. "But how are we going to find the treasure? The archaeologist is not talking, and we searched the shop the old woman spoke of, but we have not found the boy! This was all part of your brilliant plan, no?"

Dunleavey stopped abruptly, nearly getting

run over by a nanny pushing a large pram. He waited till she rerouted around him. He earned a fairly nasty look from the young woman who obviously felt she had the right-of-way. Once she pushed on, he spoke.

"We don't know for certain the boy isn't there! If you hadn't been so incredibly clumsy and knocked over the fireplace guard, we might have had more time to look. Instead, we had to get out of there before the owner came to investigate!"

Sandoval shrugged sheepishly. "What do we do now?"

A siren whined somewhere in the distance. Sandoval was unaware that Dunleavey had deliberately kicked one of the glowing red embers from the shop hearth into a stack of papers. A malevolent grin spread across Dunleavey's face.

"Let's just say the Captain has lit the smoking lamp. Any moment now the little rodents should come scurrying out. The trap is set. All we need to do is pounce."

"The Wizard of West Bow? I've never heard

of him," Rory said.

"Thomas Weir and his sister were righteous members of their church. Later, it was discovered they participated in some really awful crimes. His sister claimed that they had inherited magical powers from their witch mother. The Major, she said, was a powerful wizard. They lived not too far from here, down from the Castle, at No. 10, West Bow."

"Well, that's got to be the next stop on the trail! To No. 10 West Bow we go then!" Rory declared. Bogey wrinkled his nose.

"You smell that?"

Mad Dog sniffed the air like an eager bull mastiff. "Smells like Old Man Oxfam's smoking."

Smout frowned. "Mr. Oxfam doesn't smoke."

An orange flash of fur rocketed past the children and vaulted onto the table with a frightened hiss. The children screamed. The cat on the table yowled right back.

"Flint?" Smout laughed, and gathered the mewling feline into his arms. "Relax, everyone. It's just Mr. Oxfam's cat, remember? He told us he was probably nosing about chasing mice."

"Was he barbecuing them, too?" Bogey asked. "Because I definitely smell smoke. A lot of it. And is anyone else getting a bit warm?"

Smout suddenly remembered something else Mr. Oxfam had said about the cat.

And fire.

"Oh, no!" With an abrupt spring, Smout rushed headlong up toward the entrance of the shop. He had only reached the top of the stairs when licks of orange blocked his path. The shop was ablaze!

As the others piled to a stop behind Smout, Flint the Cat clawed furiously. His nails dug painfully into Smout's shoulder. The terrified cat launched himself to the floor and shot off in the opposite direction of the flames. Smout hoped the cat would be okay. Right now, he was more concerned for Mr. Oxfam.

"Mr. Oxfam! Mr. Oxfam! Are you okay?" His small voice was swallowed by the growing roar of the flames. The others joined in.

"Mr. Oxfam! Mr. Oxfam!"

They strained, listening for a reply. None came.

Tendrils of wicking flames writhed like serpents. They slithered nearer and nearer to the frightened children. A growing wall of fire blocked the path to the front door, eagerly consuming the defenseless stacks of books.

Fear mired their feet as surely as quicksand. Smout's eyes watered against the blinding smoke. Coupled with the heat, his weak lungs began to protest. His breaths started to strangle.

"Mr. Oxfam, please!" He managed a last, feeble cry before Rory yanked him abruptly away from the threatening flames.

"Let's get out of here!" Rory yelled. The frightened group of children was only too happy to oblige.

They tore first down one alley of bookshelves, then another. Rory led them on a mad dash through the maze of shelves, trying desperately to find some means of escape. They rounded the corner and skidded to a stop. They were back in the corner with the small table and the pebbled-glass window. The window!

Fergus Oxfam's head suddenly popped through the open frame. "Come on! Step to!"

Flint the Cat peeked over Oxfam's shoulder, yowling urgently. Oxfam pushed him off and waved urgently to the children.

"Up you go, unless you fancy yourself a crisp." He didn't need to urge them further.

Rory scrambled atop the small table, their ladder to freedom, and was the first through the window. He turned to pull the others up and through. First, he pulled Emma up through the small opening. Then Bogey. Both Bogey and Rory grabbed Mad Dog's massive arms as he mounted the tiny table. Their faces reddened with the strain of hefting the big boy's muscular weight.

"Hurry up!" Mad Dog ordered anxiously. The two boys heaved with all their might, but the large boy wedged in the window's small frame.

The beams in the ceiling began to groan. Smout cast nervous glances above his head. If they didn't get out before the beam gave way, there would be no escape. Their quest would end here in a fiery inferno, and the location of Charlie's gold would remain a mystery.

In a sudden surge of desperation, Smout climbed upon the table and leveraged himself under the flailing Mad Dog. With all his remaining strength, he pushed his friend upward until he popped through the window into the street outside. The combined weight of the two boys was too much for the rickety table to bear. The legs gave way with a loud crack. Smout tumbled to the floor.

He choked on the smoky air. His head began to swim. His vision began to dim.

"Smout!" his friends cried. They couldn't reach him. Smout lay in a crumpled, immobile heap.

"Quick! Grab my legs!" Rory ordered Mad Dog. Mad Dog realized instantly what Rory had in mind. The bully and the athlete, normally so at odds, worked together to lower Rory down through the window. He linked his arms around the lifeless Smout.

"Give a tug!" Rory yelled. Mad Dog dug in his heels and hoisted, the muscles in his biceps bulging. Just as the old wooden beam collapsed in a flurry of fiery sparks and burning wood, Smout's feet disappeared through the open window.

They scrambled across the street, collapsing against the wall of a nearby shop, panting. They watched in silence as the fire consumed the little bookstore. Finally, Bogey spoke.

"I didn't even get my shortbreads."

Rory and Mad Dog simultaneously slapped the back of his head.

CHAPTER TWENTY-SEVEN

High & Dry

The tanned pocketbook behind the glass was stamped in gold, ordinary enough.

The extraordinary disgust of the five children, however, reflected back at them as they read the information card below.

"It's made of his skin?" Mad Dog mumbled. Smout nodded wordlessly.

"From his left hand. William Burke. One of the infamous 'Resurrection Men'," Rory whispered.

They stood silent inside the small room on the

ground floor of the Police Centre. Groups of curious tourists meandered through the tiny museum maintained by the Lothian and Borders Police. The old woman behind the counter smiled at each group as they passed kindly offering information on the cleverly arranged exhibits. She seemed quite knowledgeable on all the pieces, including the vast array of truncheons fanning out across the wall.

Of course, everyone wanted to see the infamous skin purse and she was equally happy to point out the ghoulish curiosity.

The bright blue façade of the building on High Street invited locals and visitors alike to explore the history of the Edinburgh police force. It also maintained a working police service for anyone needing to report a crime, missing pets, or for those simply seeking information on how to get to the Scotch Whisky Experience.

Inspector Markham rubbed his temple as he shuttled the reluctant children past the exhibits and toward the upstairs offices. Once he began the questioning, he suddenly wished with fervor that he could go to the Scotch Whisky Experience.

The din that exploded was a roaring clamor of excited voices. Inspector Markham and Sergeant MacGregor tried to sift through the excited babble of the sooty children sitting before them. Only a few intelligible words filtered through, each one more fantastic than the next.

"...kidnapped..."

"...pirate..."

"...rotten thief..."

"...walk the plank!"

"Walk the plank?" Markham's eyebrows took off like the wings of an American Great Horned Owl. Rory smacked the back of Bogey's head.

"Thanks for putting that one in, mate."

Bogey shrugged. Truth to tell, however, the recent brush with death had loosened all their tongues on the subject of their recent escapades. All, that is, save Smout.

He sat apart from the others, huddled very small in the grey woolen blanket a medic had wrapped round his shoulders at the scene. Inspector

Markham and Sergeant MacGregor had arrived soon after, having heard the dispatch on the police band. They had taken them here, the closest police station. Traffic had rendered it impossible to get back to the main offices on Fettes Avenue. Markham hated tourist season.

Now, here they all sat, trying to answer questions on how they became separated from their chaperone and what in the name of St. Giles did they think they were about?

"We were after Bonnie Prince Charlie's gold," Mad Dog offered.

The station fell into a sudden hush.

Thus far no one had breathed a word about their quest for the treasure. Now, the cat was out of the bag, and it was meowing louder than Fergus Oxfam's mad tabby.

Smout's eyes narrowed to thin slits. His small hands balled into angry fists. Crimson flushed his pale cheeks. Just as he looked like a teapot about to boil over, Mr. Dunleavey burst into the room.

"Oh, thank goodness everyone is all alright!

I've been beside myself with worry! Whatever were you thinking, taking off like that?"

He ruffled Rory's hair and pinched Bogey's cheeks. He tutted over Emma and nearly enveloped Mad Dog in a wide embrace but the big boy growled. Dunleavey backed away a few steps and smiled awkwardly. Smout noticed a small, white bandage over Dunleavey's left eye. Before he could ponder it further, Dunleavey clapped his hands together.

"Thank you ever so much for locating the children, Inspector. Now, if we're all done here, the rector is anxiously awaiting their return to the Academy."

Inspector Markham was not in the mood to be steamrolled. The excitement in the city streets for the pending Tattoo had been building all day, along with his blood pressure. He pushed himself away from the desk and stood, a solid five inches over Dunleavey - seven if you counted the hair.

"Mr. Dunleavey?"

Dunleavey gulped audibly. "Yes, Inspector."

The Inspector crooked a finger. "Let's have a

chat, shall we?"

"Certainly!" Dunleavey squeaked. He pulled a kerchief from his pocket and dabbed at the perspiration beading on his forehead. He walked down the hall in the direction of the inspector's outstretched hand. The inspector fell in directly behind him. Sergeant MacGregor turned to the children.

"You lot stay put, right? You've caused enough trouble for one day." He hurried after the inspector.

Smout suddenly launched at Mad Dog. "You duffer! You rotter!" He pummeled the large boy with rabid fury. It took several minutes of combined effort from Rory and Bogey to pry Smout from his surprised victim.

"Geroff, mate! Are you mad!" Mad Dog scrambled backward.

Smout's breaths came long and hard. "My uncle's only chance was us finding that treasure, and you just went and blew it, you squealer!"

Emma reached out a calming hand to steady

Smout's trembling arm. "Let's be realistic, Smout. What were the chances that we could have really found the treasure? A group of silly school children? That's if there really was any treasure to begin with."

Smout was more disgusted than he'd been at the sight of Burke's skin purse.

"Of course there's a treasure. There's got to be a treasure."

"Why?" Bogey asked. "Why does there have to be a treasure? Because you say so? You're not our leader, you know."

"No. I suppose not," Smout reluctantly agreed. How silly he'd been, supposing the lot of them were his friends. Who'd want to be friends with him, after all?

"But, if there's no treasure, then I don't know how I'm supposed to get my uncle back and then," his voice trailed off. He suddenly felt very, very small. "Then, I'll have no one."

Not a soul spoke for several minutes. Finally, Rory broke the silence.

"It's better than being dead, mate."

Emma agreed. "We need to get back to the Academy. School will be letting out soon and our parents will start to worry. You need to let the police do their job. Let them find your uncle."

Smout looked up at her. "And if they don't?"

He looked at each one in turn. To a man, or in Emma's case, girl, they each looked away. Smout's shoulders fell. He hung his head, defeated. He began to absentmindedly rearrange the items on the desk where Sergeant MacGregor's had been sitting. He paused at the open notebook where the Sergeant had written a list of letters and numbers. There was also a funny little drawing doodled in the corner of the page. Smout squinted. The sketch looked remarkably like the Inspector. Except for the enormous clown shoes, of course. Smout closed the notepad.

He slumped into MacGregor's chair. He winced when something jabbed into his leg. Reaching into his pocket, he pulled out the book his uncle had ordered for him. He smiled then frowned as he wondered if this was possibly the last book he'd ever receive from his uncle. Sadness tempered the edges of his smile.

He looked at the title again. *The Wrong Box*. If Smout recalled correctly, Robert Louis Stevenson had written the story with his stepson, Lloyd. He tried to recall the plot. Something about a large sum of money and mixed up deliveries.

A thought began to nibble round the edges of his mind. He gave the book a closer inspection. The hardback book wasn't a particularly old edition. It was nice, but certainly not worth a king's ransom.

He flipped through the book. Nothing unusual fell from the pages.

The fleeting hope he had begun to feel dissipated rapidly. He began to close the book when his finger snagged on an endpaper at the back. Curious, he examined the back cover. The fire at the shop, it seemed, had loosened the glue holding the endpaper fast. Smout worried at the frayed corner with his nail, exposing a folded piece of paper hidden beneath. His face flushed with hope.

He looked around the room. When he was certain no one was looking, he freed the scrap from its hiding place. Unfolding it, he could see instantly it was another piece of the map!

Another bit of coastline snaked around the left edge of the scrap. Lines marking the depth of surrounding waters radiated out from the word "island". Smout's stomach knotted with excitement. The treasure was on an island! Loads of islands dotted the waters around Scotland. Maybe it was buried on one of them!

He flipped the piece of paper over.

Written on the back some sort of code. The series of numbers and letters looked strangely familiar. Suddenly, Smout nearly fell out of the chair.

"Smout!"

"Are you okay?"

He ignored the concerned queries and hurriedly flipped through Sergeant MacGregor's notepad. There it was! One of the numbers on the policeman's list matched the code on the back of the map!

Smout could hear the voices of the Inspector and Mr. Dunleavey coming from down the hall. He had to hurry!

"What are you doing?" Rory whispered tersely. "You're going to get pinched!"

Smout took a deep breath. He squared skinny shoulders. "If none of you will help me, I'll find Charlie's gold myself. Uncle Bernie is counting on me. I'm not going to let him down!"

With that, he stormed down the stairs, past the helpful old woman behind the counter, and exploded through the glass-paned door and into the growing excitement on the outside street.

CHAPTER TWENTY-SEVEN

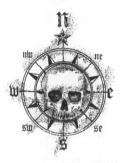

Scuppered

Bluidy had absolutely no idea where his son and ragtag group of friends might be, or his brother Bernie, for that matter. But, he had a clear notion of some people who did.

Bluidy and Mr. Grey had spent the better part of an hour combing the Edinburgh streets for the gawky secretary and the odd-looking Spaniard. Bluidy was almost certain the pair was working together to locate and steal the treasure. It was much too coincidental to believe the Spaniard's visit to the museum and Dunleavey's attempted attack on Smout were not related. They undoubtedly had a hand in his brother's disappearance as well.

He and Mr. Grey headed for the train station. When they arrived, Mr. Grey spotted Dunleavey's coat almost instantly. Only, it wasn't Dunleavey wearing the tailored jacket. Mr. Grey yanked the homeless man out of the bin in which he been rummaging.

"Hang on! What's this?" he cried, dangling from Mr. Grey's grasp like a wriggling worm on a hook. "I was just looking for a bit of nosh is all."

Bluidy nodded to Mr. Grey. The leviathan set the man down gently. Bluidy pulled his wallet from his pocket and fished out a five pound note. He started to hand it to the man, who greedily held out his hands. The old man's tongue licked his dry, cracked lips. At the last moment, however, Bluidy yanked back the bill.

"I tell you what," he began. "The fiver's yours if you can tell me where you got that coat."

The bum tugged on his lapels. "A proper gentleman passed it on, he did. Took a fancy to me coat. Traded him for it fair and square. Then he left."

"Did you see which way he went?"

The man nodded. "The bobbies shuttled me out the station. Heard him on his mobile. Dribbled something about books."

"Books?" Bluidy pressed. "Was he talking about a library? A newsagent? A bookstore?" The pitch of each query pitched in urgency.

The man scowled, deciding perhaps that the five pounds wasn't worth such trouble. He looked up at Mr. Grey and, in a rare moment of bravery, decided to risk it, and began to walk away.

"A tenner, then!" Bluidy called out. The man stopped. He turned back to Bluidy, shuffled forward, and cleared his throat.

"The gentleman in question might have mentioned a shop. Gubbins Corner, if memory serves. Over on Lawnmarket."

He cleanly plucked the paper note from Bluidy outstretched hand. "Pleasure doing business with you, gentlemen." He tipped his hand in a jaunty salute and shuffled along, buoyed at his good fortune. He smiled. And his father had said he had no marketable skills.

Mixed-up deliveries. Smout knew exactly why Uncle Bernie had given him *The Wrong Box*. It was all about mix-ups.

The children had solved Uncle Bernie's musical clue. Trouble was they had supposed it referred to Major Thomas Weir, the Wizard of West Bow. But they had gotten their weirs mixed-up! The weir they should have gotten to was *The Weir of Hermiston*! Stevenson's last novel, the one he had been working on the morning of his death, was all about Archie Weir, the estranged son of the Lord Justice Clerk. Archie, like Stevenson, had attended the University of Edinburgh. The University boasted several spectacular museums, like the Talbot Rice Gallery and the Reid Concert Hall Museum of Instruments. Smout recalled seeing a particularly wicked-looking pipe there in the shape of an ebony serpent when he'd visited the museum with his music class on school field trip. But what interested Smout now was the university's extensive library. The code on the back of the last scrap of map was a catalogue number from a library, and Smout was betting it came from a book at the school Stevenson and the fictitious Archie had attended.

He ducked in between the people making their way up the High Street. He hurried past Parliament Square and the statue of Adam Smith where an American family was posing for snaps. The Loch Ness monster swam across the father's stomach, dancing across the stomach rolls of his wide "I Saw Nessie" t-shirt. Smout paused for just a moment, momentarily envying the sticky toddler protesting in the mother's arms. He shook himself from his reverie. He had no time to waste.

He was a wanted man.

Any moment now, the Inspector would realize he'd gone missing and would give chase. All hopes of finding the treasure would go up like the brilliant fireworks that would fly over the Castle tonight. He pressed through the growing crowd, quickening his pace. It shouldn't have taken him long to get to the University library, but he still hadn't recovered fully from inhaling all that smoke. He had already begun to wheeze. How did he ever hope to cover the distance in time? What he needed was a magic carpet, he thought dismally. Unfortunately, he was in Edinburgh, not Agrabah.

At that very moment, a cheery beep sounded behind him. He turned to see the Finn Transportation Fleet pulling alongside him. Finn Fraser hung from the window and gave a hearty wave.

"Well, cheers, mate! Don't suppose you need a ride, eh?"

Smout grinned.

The jovial old woman was in the middle of explaining the history of an over-large walkie-talkie to a group of German tourists when Inspector Markham's baritone rattled the glass on the Burke display case.

"He what!"

For the first time since she began working for

the Centre, the old woman stopped smiling.

The German tourists immediately excused themselves with hastily mumbled *auf wiedersehens*. On the upper floor of the station, the Inspector paced the floor, his hands waving wildly over the heads of the remaining children.

"What do you mean he's gone off?" the Inspector railed. "Weren't you instructed to stay put?" The children nodded wordlessly. Markham turned to his subordinate officer. "Didn't you tell them to stay put, MacGregor?"

The Sergeant nodded as well. "I was very explicit in the details, sir. 'You lot stay put.' Can't see as how I could have been any clearer, sir." He narrowed a withering stare at the children who huddled as far from the disgruntled police as the small offices would allow.

Dunleavey, however, remained remarkably calm. While in interrogation, the cunning secretary had made a bold move. He had told the truth.

Well, part of it, anyway. He had let slip certain details about Bluidy's mad search for the lost fortune of Bonnie Prince Charlie. He had explained how Bluidy believed Bernie McManus had information that would lead to the treasure and had unwisely passed it along to his nephew, placing the boy in danger.

He just left out the part where he admitted *he* was the danger.

"Well, such a small boy, he can't have gone far. Why don't I take the rest of the children back to school now, Inspector? Get them out of your way, so you can concentrate on finding the lad?" He gripped Bogey firmly by both shoulders.

The ruffled Inspector leveled a probing stare at the wiry secretary. His infamous gut was roiling, but he couldn't decide if it was the boy's disappearance, his uncle's, or the steady calm of the peculiar secretary that gave him the sudden desire to reach for the calcium bicarbonate. Indecision wasn't aiding forward progress, he thought, however. Finally, he nodded.

"Very well. Take the children back to the Academy. I expect their parents will be glad to have them back safe and sound."

"Absolutely," Dunleavey heartily agreed.

"Don't suppose he let it slip where he's headed?" the Inspector asked, turning to the children. Dunleavey squeezed his talons into Bogey's shoulders, very nearly drawing blood. Bogey winced, letting out a sharp yip.

Bogey caught the startled gaze of the other children. He shook his head at them. The motion was nearly imperceptible to anyone else in the room, but the children immediately received the message.

"No, sir, Inspector. Not a clue," Rory answered.

Inspector Markham eyeballed the tall lad, trying to detect any subterfuge. His stomach burbled like a MacBeth cauldron, but the boy seemed to be telling the truth.

"We should get going then," Dunleavey suggested. "Yes, we've taken up far too much of the good Inspector's valuable time. Come along children." He shuffled the small group down to the ground floor. The old woman waved a friendly farewell, but Dunleavey could not be bothered. He rushed the children to a sedan lingering near the curb just outside the station. He urged them all inside the car quickly then took a position in the front next to Arturo Sandoval. He nodded quickly to the Spaniard. Sandoval put the car in gear and headed west toward St. Giles Street. The children remained in the back seat, huddled in frightened silence as they passed through a roundabout, made a quick jog to the right then came out on Canongate. Holyrood Palace loomed regally in the distance. Finally, Emma screwed up enough courage to speak.

"Where are you taking us, Mr. Dunleavey? This isn't the way to the school."

"I'm well aware of that, young lady," Dunleavey responded without turning. He muttered an order to Sandoval in Spanish, who nodded.

Suddenly, Dunleavey turned to face the four frightened children. Gone was the sniveling, awkward assistant to the rector. In his place was a man sick with fever. Gold fever. His eyes burned as he leaned into the children.

"Now, before I have to get nasty, where is our young friend heading, hm?"

Finn and Smout had also headed left from the Police Centre. Finn's taxi, however, took the second left at the George IV Bridge and headed south. As they passed the National Museum of Scotland, Finn regaled Smout with spine-tingling tales of the Arthur's Seat coffins. Found in 1836 by five small boys not unlike Smout himself, the tiny wooden coffins and the carved wooden figures inside each were supposed to represent the seventeen victims of Burke and Hare, Edinburgh's infamous murdering duo.

"Leastaways, that's what some folks think. You heard of them? The Resurrection Men?" Finn asked.

"Yeah," Smout replied. "As a matter of fact, I just saw a pocketbook made from Burke's skin."

Finn whirled around to stare at Smout. "Caw! Are you serious?"

"Finn!" Smout yelled as Finn's taxi drifted.

The boy gestured wildly through the windscreen at the oncoming traffic barreling toward them. Anxious horns pealed into the afternoon. Finn righted their course, turning down Potterow.

"That's just not right," the scruffy driver noted. "Aw, well. Suppose he got what he deserved anyhow. Hung from the gallows for all to see. Spot's right by St. Giles. Even marked it in the ground proper with brass markers. In the shape of an 'H'."

Finn let go of the wheel once more to demonstrate the shape of the letter. The taxi snaked dangerously with no guidance. Smout jabbed his finger forward yet again. He had the fleeting thought that he'd survived the fire only to perish in an auto crash.

At the last moment, Finn righted the taxi and pressed on. "All these buggers headed for the Castle and the opening of the Tattoo. That's why I came into the city, you know. Was hardly a soul in Port Edgar. Only fares I had all morning was you lot and the gent with the cane. Picked him up outside the train station. Asked to come all the way into town.

Was a decent fare and figured I could catch a few others from the tourists if I was lucky."

A cane, Smout worried. It had to be Bluidy. He was back in the city. Smout knew he would have to be careful. At least the others were back safe with Mr. Dunleavey.

As they turned onto Buccleuch Place, the library rose eight stories to Smout's right. To his left, the Meadows spread wide and green. A few lads sparred in a spirited football match. Smout recalled attending a Hearts-Hibs match with Uncle Bernie last year. He had explained how the fierce rivalry between Edinburgh's most beloved teams began in 1875 when the two met in the first derby. Finn's voice brought Smout back to the present.

"Your destination, sir." Smout opened the rusty taxi door. It groaned in protest. After the wild ride with Finn, Smout's stomach groaned as well.

As he stepped from the car, Finn called out. "If you don't mind me asking, lad, what is it you're looking for here, anyway?"

Smout turned. "A book, of course."

Finn stared blankly. It was quite clear the only book he was familiar with took bets on the Edinburgh Cup. After a brief moment or two, he waved cheerily, and sputtered off, leaving noxious clouds of blackened petrol fumes in his wake.

Smout watched the gypsy cab pull away, slightly saddened to see Finn go. He knew he was brave enough to handle this dangerous quest on his own. That didn't mean he had to like it.

He turned toward the building. Large letters, nearly two-feet tall, announced the building's use as a library for curious passers-by. Each story had large windows overlooking the Meadows. Smout supposed it was to give students something pleasant to look at when their eyes tired of scanning endless lines of scholarly text.

He noticed a portly uniformed gentleman standing near the library entrance, checking identification of the people walking into the library. A guard?

Smout began to worry. Had it been the middle of term, he might have been able to sneak past, losing himself in a sea of students frantic to complete overdue essays. During the summer months however, the library traffic was thin, at best. Smout had no idea what he was going to do, but he had to get into the library! The next clue was in there, and Uncle Bernie's time was running out.

"You look like you need some assistance."

The voice behind him turned Smout's blood to icy slurry. It was Bluidy.

CHAPTER TWENTY-EIGHT

Staying the Course

The ruins of Holyrood Abbey rose like a skeleton rising out of the past. The grey spires of the crumbling nave wall resembled so many spindly vertebrae. Stone buttresses stretching out from the sides of the nave looked like the bony ribs of a sleeping giant. The tall, empty frame of the once-glorious stained glass window was an eyeless skull staring vacantly over the grave memorials of Stewarts who long ago crumbled into skulls and bones themselves.

The Abbey, like so many of Edinburgh's buildings and monuments, had a history. Mary, Queen of Scots, one of the most controversial rulers of Scots history, had worshipped here. Emma shuddered as she remembered studying about the violent assassination of Mary's secretary, David Rizzio, in the Queen's supper chamber. Supposedly, one could still make out the stain of the young man's blood on the wooden floor. Emma supposed that was a bunch of hooey for the tourists, but as Dunleavey shoved her smartly between the shoulders, Emma wished heartily a certain other secretary might meet a similar demise.

She hadn't meant to give away the Wizard of West Bow clue, but the beady-eyed man had frightened her so when he had grabbed her arm in the car and twisted. Rory had nearly caused the sedan to crash when he had leapt to her rescue. He had succeeded in fighting the thin man off, but the respite was brief. They were still his prisoners.

"Keep moving!" Dunleavey growled. The thin man walked behind the tightly grouped formation

269

of children while Arturo Sandoval waddled along in front. Emma supposed they looked like another class on field trip, but truth was, when Sandoval pulled into the Palace car park, the children had no idea where they were being taken. Sandoval led them past the Abbey proper and over the grass toward the public walk heading up Arthur's Seat. Soon, they were out of sight of the warden who was just about to lead another hourly tour of the Abbey. Emma stumbled on an uneven rock. Rory reached out and caught her by the elbow.

"Thanks."

Rory smiled. "No problem."

Sandoval led them off the marked path. Suddenly, he disappeared right before their eyes, consumed by the mountain.

"How's that?" Mad Dog rubbed his eyes. Then, as quickly as he had disappeared, Sandoval rematerialized.

"Here it is. Come quickly."

"Where are we going?" Bogey whispered.

"I've no clue," Rory replied.

"Do you suppose he's going to, well, you know." Bogey made a slicing motion across his throat and gulped.

Rory shook his head. "Don't think so. If he were going to off us, there are better places to do it."

"You mean like a dark, mysterious tunnel that seems to go on forever and ever?" Mad Dog interjected.

"Exactly."

Mad Dog pointed. As Dunleavey led the children behind the boulder, they realized it was a natural *trompe l'oeil,* an illusion of perspective. From their original angle, all they could see was a large boulder leaning against a crag of the mountain. Solid and impassable. However, if one simply shifted one's perspective a bit to the left there was, just as Mad Dog had described, the yawning mouth of a dark tunnel cut into the jagged face of the mountain.

"Inside!" Dunleavey ordered before anyone could protest. One by one, the mountain swallowed them whole, and darkness enveloped them.

Sandoval turned on a torch and played the

beam on the stony floor of the tunnel. He shone the bright column down the tunnel path where it was consumed by the blackness.

"This way."

The children looked nervously at one another. Finally, Mad Dog gestured to Emma.

"Ladies first," he laughed weakly.

Smout tried to decide. Should he run, or should he scream? What Bluidy said next stopped him dead in his tracks.

"Victoria would be very proud of you."

The mention of his mother's name brought a flurry of mixed feelings to the surface, a peculiar mix of pride and sadness. Smout swallowed the sadness and looked warily at Bluidy.

"What do you know about my mother?"

A crooked smile cracked the harsh line of Bluidy's mouth. "A great deal, actually. I suppose you could say we were, well, partners."

Smout's eyes narrowed. Bluidy could see Smout's hesitation. He needed to give Smout the information slowly. Gain the lad's trust.

"She was a brilliant researcher. A great history detective. Like you."

Smout's instincts began to tingle. He already suspected Bluidy was involved in his uncle's disappearance. He wondered if he had something to do with his mother's as well.

"Oh, yeah? Did you try to knock her over the head like you nearly did me?"

Bluidy knelt in front of Smout. "No, no, dear boy. I would never do anything to hurt your mother, or you. I was trying to protect you back at the train station. That rascal Dunleavey was behind you. He was the one trying to hurt you. Not me."

Smout took a moment to consider what Bluidy was saying. True, he couldn't recall seeing the weasely secretary after he had excused himself in Port Edgar. And the children had spilled the beans about the gold back at the Stevenson house. Then he remembered. The police station. The bandage over Dunleavey's eye. It hadn't been there before the Dalmeny train station. Perhaps Bluidy was telling the truth. Smout decided to try another question.

"Do you know where my uncle is?"

Bluidy shook his head. "But, I'm fairly certain our Mr. Dunleavey does. He most likely kidnapped your uncle to try and get him to reveal the location of the treasure."

Smout started. "There's no way Uncle Bernie would talk! He'd rather die than see a fiend like Dunleavey get his hands on a treasure that rightfully belongs to Scotland."

The gravity of his statement began to sink in.

Bluidy saw his opening. He nodded solemnly. "Aye. That's what I fear. Unless we can find the treasure first, I fear for your uncle's safety."

Smout almost spilled everything. He nearly told Bluidy about the mysterious package Uncle Bernie had sent him, the package that had started this whole madcap dash through the city. He almost told him about the map and the clues when something suddenly gave him pause.

"How did you know where to find me?" Smout asked warily, the muscles in his legs poising for flight.

"Mr. Grey and I ran into one of Mr. Dunleavey's associates at your uncle's offices at the museum. That's how we came into possession of the Louis d'Or. We, er, persuaded him to part ways with it."

"You *stole* it from him."

"Yes, I'm afraid so. But for all the right reasons! Surely, such an important piece of history needed to be protected."

Smout was still leery. "Surely."

"At any rate, there was an odd list of numbers on your uncle's desk. Any researcher worth his salt could recognize them as library catalogue numbers. We expected the trail might lead to one of the libraries in the city. We tried the National Library first, of course. When you weren't there, we came directly here. And now, here you are. Makes sense, of course."

"Of course." Smout was relieved. It did make sense. Perhaps Bluidy wasn't the selfish tomb raider he'd originally taken him for. Dunleavey was the real enemy.

A frightening thought suddenly occurred to Smout.

"My friends! I left them. Back at the police station. With Dunleavey!"

Bluidy's face grew somber. "That is troublesome. That makes it all the more urgent we find the treasure quickly."

Smout decided. He would only tell Bluidy what he needed to know. He would keep the pieces of the map secret. He pointed toward the guard at the library entrance.

"I need to get into that library. I think I know where to look."

Bluidy arched one eyebrow. "Really, now?"

"Yes, but children aren't allowed in without an adult. Get me in, and we'll talk."

Bluidy stepped aside to let Smout lead. "After you, sir."

CHAPTER THIRTY

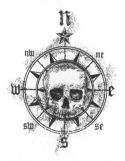

The Resurrection Men

It felt as though they had been walking forever. The torch's beam only illuminated a few metres in front of them, and the rough hewn ground was uneven at best. Emma stumbled frequently. Her knees were caked with blood and tears had begun to streak her dirty cheeks. Finally, Rory reached out a steadying hand, and now they walked, side-by-side, her hand enveloped in his. Bogey was a bundle of live nerves. He babbled on about the ghosts rumored to haunt the underground vaults and tunnels like this.

He prattled on about Annie, the ghost of the little girl in rags with long dirty hair, who cried because she had lost her doll.

"You don't suppose we'll run into her, do you?" he had asked. "Not like she can hurt us, right?"

"She probably won't, but if you don't zipper up, I just might," Mad Dog snarled back, but he let the younger boy hang on tightly to the tail of his shirt anyway.

Soon, a glowing sliver could be seen wavering in the distance. It grew brighter as they got closer, signaling an end to their underground trek. They slipped through a gap similar to the one they had used to enter the underground tunnel. They entered a cavernous room lit by dim lantern light.

The robot stood sentinel in the center of the room, waiting patiently for its chance to find a treasure. The children looked around first in awe then in cold fear. Dunleavey shoved them toward an iron-barred cell.

"In you go!" he ordered as Sandoval opened

the door wide. Emma screamed as a dirty, ragged figure ripped from the shadows on the opposite side of the cell and bolted at them.

"It's the ghost of Annie!" Bogey screamed.

Rory threw himself in between Emma and the attacker.

"Back away!" Rory warned.

It was no ghost. A very real flesh and blood human grabbed them by the shoulders, each one in turn and asked, "Smout? Are you Smout? Where's Smout?"

"He's not here! Now, bugger off!" Mad Dog snapped.

The stranger shuffled quietly back his corner and slumped against the stone wall. A resounding clang echoed as Sandoval secured the great metal door of their prison. The startled children jumped.

"Now, you stay put," Dunleavey began. "Can't have you running off to warn the Inspector now, can we?" He smiled coldly. "Enjoy your new quarters. I'm afraid there is no maid service, so mind the mess. As for me, well, I'm off to see the Wizard."

He laughed at his own joke. "Of course, in my story, the Yellow Brick Road is paved in gold. Charlie's gold. And it's all mine. Goodbye, then." The children watched as Dunleavey disappeared through the concealed exit.

As for Sandoval, he giggled maniacally then maneuvered a few keys on the computer keyboard. The robot clacked its menacing hook in a crude, but threatening farewell wave. Sandoval giggled again then squeezed through the concealed exit and disappeared leaving them alone.

Rory turned to the dark figure crouched quietly in the corner. The boy took a cautious step forward. "You're Uncle Bernie, aren't you?"

"Very perceptive, young man. Yes, I am Bernard McManus." The dirty figure stepped into the wavering light. "Well, would that we'd met under better circumstances, but, welcome to the Edinburgh Castle dungeons."

"*The Oxford Nursery Rhyme Book*," Smout announced. "That's the book we're looking for." He looked up from the computer's catalogue screen.

They had gotten past the guard and the front desk with something called an ELP. Smout had never heard of it.

"Edinburgh Libraries Passport," Bluidy explained. "An ELP."

Smout was duly impressed. Anyone who had a passport to use any library in and around Edinburgh couldn't be all that bad. Still, he felt safer keeping the revelation of the map and the clues to himself for awhile. He was certain Bluidy was not telling him everything.

Well, two could play at that game.

"How do you know that's the right book? There was a whole list of numbers," Bluidy asked.

"Call it a hunch. Come on. It's on the third floor."

They took the elevator. Smout quickly checked the decimal numbers posted on the end of each shelf row, searching for the proper sequence that would lead them to the book they wanted. Finding the correct row, he dashed through the stacks, running an eager finger along the spines to find his quarry.

"Aha!" he cried.

He fished a thin volume from the shelf and brought it to the study table where Bluidy sat waiting. He placed the book on the table's flat surface and sat across from Bluidy, laying his hands flat on either side of the book. Bluidy smiled and gave a nod.

"Go ahead. You do it."

Smout grinned widely and grabbed the book. He looked through the index of titles and first lines, searching for a clue. Then he saw it. That had to be it! He turned to the proper page. There it was. Another piece of the map! He was getting closer!

It was a corner piece. A few more lines angled across the face along with the portion of a ship. The word "Savannah" was clearly legible near the bottom. He was just about to see if Uncle Bernie had left another clue on the back when Bluidy's voice startled him. He nearly lost the paper.

"What's that you have there?" Bluidy asked, craning his neck forward. Smout quickly tucked the scrap into his pocket.

"What? Oh, nothing. Someone's just left a bit of notepaper as a bookmark or something. Here's something, though. This book has an old rhyme called *St. Ives* in it."

"That's a riddle rhyme, isn't it? As I was traveling to St. Ives," Bluidy began.

Smiling, Smout picked up the rhyme. "I met a man with seven wives. Each wife had seven sacks."

"Each sack had seven cats. Each cat had seven kits."

"Kits, cats, sacks, wives..."

"How many were going to St. Ives!" Bluidy and Smout finished together. Smout bounced excitedly in his chair.

"I know this one! In fact, that's it! That's the answer. One!" Then he sat back frowning, puzzled. "What do you suppose it means?"

"Hm," Bluidy began. "Stevenson wrote a novel called *St. Ives*. Perhaps we should find a copy. I'm certain the library has one. I'll go look."

Smout nodded eagerly.

As soon as Bluidy was out of sight, he stole a

glance at the back of the scrap he'd just found. It was another rhyme, but this was no Mother Goose.

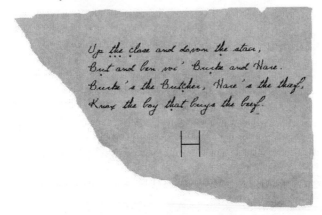

Burke and Hare! The Resurrection Men! Of course! The horrifying exploits of the two historical grave robbers gave inspiration to Stevenson's *The Body Snatchers*. A small capital "H" appeared beneath the rhyme. A recollection itched at Smout's memory. Hadn't Finn said something about a brass "H" marking the spot where Burke had hung to his death? Maybe that's where they needed to go next.

The thump of Bluidy's cane heralded his arrival. Smout quickly stuffed the scrap back into his pocket. Bluidy strode to the table.

"Here we go. *St. Ives*. It was right on this

very floor. Fancy that. What do you say we take a look on page one?"

Of course, Smout thought. The riddle's answer most certainly was a marker meant to lead them to the first page of *St. Ives*. All of a sudden, Smout began to perspire. What was he going to do? If Bluidy opened the book and found a piece of the map, Smout's secret would be revealed. He would have to confess all he knew about Uncle Bernie's map. His brain scrambled, trying to think of a distraction. All he could think of was to snatch the book from Bluidy's hands.

"That's okay. I can do it," he squeaked like a pip mouse. His efforts to grab the book faltered. Before he could stop it, the book fell to the ground. The pages fell open to the first. What Smout saw caused his mouth to drop open in surprise.

There was nothing there!

There was something there. Detective Sergeant MacGregor was certain of it. For a man who prided himself on remembering the details, it bothered him to no end that he could not place his finger on the tiny detail that had been nagging him all day. There was something he'd seen. Something he'd heard. Something that seemed slightly out of place. But what was it?

He flipped back through his book, past his copious notes and the curious doodle of the Inspector. Nothing jumped out at him. He nearly jumped out of his skin, however, when the Inspector slammed down the phone receiver. Obviously, things had not gone well with the Superintendent. They had been about to hit the Edinburgh streets to search for the missing boy and his uncle when the call had come in. Against his better judgment, the Inspector had answered it. As he listened to the Superintendent's voice echoing shrilly through the receiver, MacGregor was suddenly very glad to be the low man on the totem pole.

"MacGregor!" the Inspector bellowed.

That was when Detective Sergeant MacGregor suddenly remembered watermelons rolled downhill. He winced. "Right here, sir."

"Refresh my memory, MacGregor. When we

started out this morning, we just had one missing person, correct? A missing archaeologist."

"Indeed, sir."

"Then by nine, we still had the missing archaeologist, but then were also missing five children, one of whom was related to the archaeologist. Is that right so far?"

"Spot on, sir."

"And let's not forget the missing secretary and the prominent business man. Let's see. What's that bring the count to, MacGregor?"

MacGregor hastily scrawled out the equation in his notepad. "One plus five equals six. Then add one, no add two, which brings the total to eight. But, don't forget, we found the children, so take away five, which brings us back to three. The archaeologist, the secretary, and the businessman."

"Ah, but by two, we had the secretary back."

"Two by two."

"But lost one of the children again."

"Three."

"Your arithmetic is flawless, MacGregor."

MacGregor smiled uncertainly, not sure how this little exercise had earned him a compliment. That's why he was less-than-surprised when the Inspector suddenly erupted.

"Then tell me why is our missing persons count now back up to eight!" The Inspector slammed his hands down on his desk, upending his coffee cup. Brown liquid began to seep across the desk. The Inspector pulled out his handkerchief and began to blot at the spill.

Something tugged at MacGregor's memory.

"Pardon me, sir?"

"That was the Superintendent. The rector from the Academy called. Dunleavey and the children never made it back. One archaeologist, five children, one secretary, and one businessman. Eight missing persons!"

Suddenly, the detail that had been nagging him sharpened into crystal clear focus. The handkerchief at Dalmeny Station. Dunleavey's handkerchief. They were identical!

"Sir?"

"What is it now, MacGregor?"

"What if Bluidy isn't our bad guy?"

"Come again?"

"What if Dunleavey lied?" He explained his theory of the handkerchief.

"Do you know what this means, MacGregor?"

"What, sir?"

"We've just released four innocent children into the custody of a kidnapper."

He could almost taste the gold. He had not gotten any assistance from the archaeologist. As for Bluidy, he had most certainly gotten in the way. Dunleavey gingerly touched the cut on his temple.

The children, however, proved to be quite a different matter. He almost giggled at how easy it had been to elicit the treasure's location from the girl.

They arrived at No. 10 West Bow, or at least where No. 10 should have been. Dunleavey leapt from the car, his eyes frantically searching the house numbers. Eighty-two, eighty-four, eighty-six...the numbers were completely wrong! All he saw was a boutique, a gallery, and a store dealing in Christmas fancies. He forced himself not to panic. Street numbers often changed over time. He grabbed the arm of a young woman heading into one of the businesses.

"No. 10 West Bow, the house of Thomas Weir. Which of these establishments is it?"

The young woman laughed. "Why, none of them, of course. That came down ages ago. In the 1800s sometime, I think."

"Are you certain? A friend told me I might find it here."

"I'm afraid your friend's played a bit of a joke on you then. How delightful. I love jokes." She chuckled again and moved into her shop, a bright orange joke and novelty shop with a huge Groucho Marx nose and mustache tickling the door frame. Dunleavey's blood began to boil.

He hated jokes.

Smout snatched the book from the floor. "Let me see that."

He rifled through the pages, searching for the bit of map he was certain should have been there. Nothing fell from the pages. He searched the text of the first page for some other kind of clue, a secret message, anything, that might point him in the right direction.

"Chapter one. A tale of a lion rampant," he read. It was useless! What had Uncle Bernie been about sending him to this book?

"Do you know what every decent treasure hunt starts with?" Bluidy's voice interrupted Smout's roiling thoughts. Smout looked toward the chair where Bluidy casually sat, legs crossed. In Bluidy's right hand, pinched between his long index finger and his thumb, he held what Smout had been searching for. Bluidy looked at the scrap in his grasp.

"It always starts with a map."

They made a curious assemblage sitting on the cold, stone floor of the cell. The children faced Smout's Uncle Bernie. All parties studied each other, drinking in the details, trying to work the pieces of the puzzle.

Rory searched Bernie's face. His leathery skin was streaked with dirt and grime, giving him an almost ruddy appearance. Bernie reminded the teenager of someone. He just couldn't remember who. Rory recalled Smout's first description of his archaeologist uncle. Rory smirked. Bernie certainly did look like someone who would seem equally at home with the pygmies of Papua New Guinea or ferreting out lost witch bottles in some grandmother's backyard.

"So, you're the one who sent Smout on his crazy treasure hunt then?" Mad Dog finally asked.

"Oh, it's not crazy at all," Bernie replied.

"Are you dotty? All those mad clues?" Mad Dog burst.

Emma nodded. "We followed them all, Mr. McManus. Not a single one led to the treasure. Just one mysterious clue after another."

"And we got ourselves kidnapped and very nearly killed," Bogey interjected.

Bernie nodded. "Yes. I am dreadfully sorry

about that. I never meant for anyone to come to harm. That was not my intent. But are you quite certain you found no treasure?"

Mad Dog guffawed. "Yeah. 'Cause if I'd found the treasure I'd be sitting around with the likes of you. In a dungeon."

"Not everything has to glitter to be gold, my young friend."

"Tell that to Bluidy," Mad Dog scoffed.

Bernie turned quickly. "Bluidy? Jack Bluidy is on the hunt as well? This is turning out better than I expected."

Bogey leaned in to Rory. He waggled his finger in small, concentric circles near his head. "Think the old boy's gone mad."

"No, no. Not mad. Delirious, perhaps. Deliriously happy."

Mad Dog whistled low. "You do realize we're trapped in a dungeon, right? And the bad guys are going to get the treasure?"

Bernie shook his head. "Oh, I doubt that very much. Not unless they know one very important thing."

"And what's that?" Bogey asked.

"Which weir is where."

Bluidy knew! Smout's hand went instinctively to the pocket that held the remaining pieces of the map. Bluidy made no move toward him. Rather, he just sat back in his chair contemplating the paper in his hand.

"You know, when I was a lad, my older brother used to set out clues for me much like this. Puzzles to be solved. Riddles to be answered. He created fantastic hunts through our house and yard that led to glorious treasures. 'Course, back then the treasures were more like a hidden bit of candy or a small toy he thought I might fancy."

"Sounds like fun," Smout replied curiously. Uncle Bernie used to do the same thing for him.

"It most certainly was. Mum was never around and even if Dad was, he couldn't be bothered. So, instead, my big brother kept me entertained. He knew I loved *Treasure Island,* so he'd spend time sketching out these wonderful maps. I imagine I fancied myself a bit like Jim Hawkins searching for Flint's treasure."

Bluidy leaned forward and handed the scrap to Smout. Smout reached out a wary hand and took the small piece of paper.

"I always imagined if I had a boy someday, I'd do the same for him."

Smout called up the memory of digging up shells on the beach with his mother and father. Bluidy had much in common with his father. Once again, Smout felt a certain kinship with the rough man. Perhaps he could trust him.

Smout fished in his pocket for the other pieces of the map.

"Mr. Bluidy? I think I have something you should see."

CHAPTER THIRTY

Pieces of Eight

"Which weir is where?" Mad Dog grumbled. "We're stuck in a dungeon. Now's not exactly the time for tongue twisters, old man."

"Oh, I love tongue twisters!" Bogey exclaimed. "Try this one three times fast! Apple mango tango. Apple mangled tango. Appled mangy tangelo. Isn't it brilliant?" He ducked before Mad Dog could smack him.

"It's not meant to be a tongue twister at all, my boy. Allow me to explain. You see, when I

296

devised my little treasure hunt, I created eight separate clues," Bernie said.

"Pieces of eight? Like pirate's gold?" Emma mused. "That's actually quite clever."

"Yes. I thought so," Bernie chuckled.

"Hold on. Eight clues? We've only located two," Rory interrupted.

Emma shook her head. "No. I expect Smout found a third. That's why he took off at the Police Centre. It was in the book, wasn't it Mr. McManus. *The Wrong Box*. That's why you had it waiting for Smout at the book shop. You knew he would eventually go there."

"Exactly right, young lady. In fact, I counted on it. You see, individually, the clues are almost worthless. Meaningless. It's like only having, well, part of a map."

Bogey grinned. "But if you put them all together, it all makes perfect sense!"

"Precisely!" Bernie agreed. "You need a tiny bit of something from each of them to appreciate the bigger picture. That was something I'd hoped my brother would understand when I sent him the letter."

"Your brother? What's your brother got to do with any of this?"

"Quite honestly? Everything."

Perhaps it was the way the lantern light flickered across Bernie's features, or it might have been a familiar glint in his eyes, but Rory shot to attention with all the surprise of a jack-in-the-box.

"Bluidy's your brother!"

The rest of the children looked at him strangely. He may as well have sprouted pink polka dots and called himself Father Christmas. Rory shook his head at them.

"Remember the photo in Smout's house? The man in the snap? Imagine him with a scar!"

Their faces tightened with the effort of recall. One by one, however, they all came to the same conclusion. The man in the picture with Smout was, in fact, Bluidy.

"Which means," Bogey reasoned, "Bluidy is Smout's dad."

"Excellent detective skills," Bernie smiled.

"Smout's found himself quite a group of friends."

"Yeah, some friends we turned out to be. He was determined, no matter what, to find the treasure and rescue you," Emma began. "We sort of let him down."

"We gave up on him," Bogey sighed.

"Now, he's out there and look where we are," Rory agreed.

A silence fell over the group. Everyone jumped in surprise when Mad Dog erupted.

"Haven't you listened to a word the man's said?" He was met by a collection of blank stares. He threw his hands up in the air.

"Caw! Now I know how you must feel half the time!" he said to Emma. He began to explain. "By themselves, the pieces are worthless, but take a tiny piece from all of them?"

Emma's eyes widened. "Mad Dog, I could positively kiss you right now!"

Mad Dog toed the ground in embarrassment as Emma continued. "What he means is, if we all work together, we can figure a way out of this!"

"Right, then!"

"Count me in!"

The flurry of excitement dissipated as Bernie frowned.

"What's wrong, Mr. McManus?" Emma asked.

Bernie began to pace the dirty prison floor. Little clouds of dust plumed in his path. His fingers worried at the straggles of hair growing on his chin. He stopped abruptly. "You gave Mr. Dunleavey the clue about Thomas Weir, correct? The Wizard of West Bow?"

Emma nodded. "I had to. I was terribly frightened. He looked so very angry."

"Not as angry as when he discovers it is a false trail, I'm afraid. Mr. Dunleavey will be back here soon, and he won't be happy. I hate to think of what he might do."

Bernie's gaze wandered to the metal robot sitting coldly on the table.

Bogey gulped. "You mean *schhhlllliiccck*?" He drew his finger slowly across his throat.

Bernie McManus nodded, mimicking Bogey's motion. "Yes. I mean exactly *schhhllliiccck.*"

The four pieces of the map were laid out upon the table surface. Bluidy and Smout had crudely fitted them together, some semblance of the whole coming through. They'd made a list of all the clues written on the pieces, looking for patterns.

"We figured they all had something to do with Robert Louis Stevenson," Smout offered. "If he really found Prince Charlie's treasure, it sort of makes sense. Doesn't it?"

"There's definitely a connection. Look how each of the clues has something to do with one or more of the others. But, look here. What's this about?" Bluidy pointed to the second piece of map the children had found, the piece containing the musical phrase. "*The key is the key.* I can't make any sense of it."

"Emma supposed it meant the musical key. You needed to know the key to solve the names of the notes."

301

"Hm. I suppose. It just seems like we're missing something."

Smout had a sudden flash of insight. Something was missing!

"The key!" he cried.

He fumbled in his pocket and pulled out the old skeleton key. "I'd nearly forgotten all about this. We found it with the first clue. In his excitement to show Bluidy the relic, he lost his grip and the key thunked on the table.

"Hold on," Smout said, picking it up. "Does that sound hollow to you?"

"It certainly does," Bluidy replied.

"Let's check it out."

Bluidy nodded eagerly. Smout examined the key closely. He gripped the skull at the top of the key and gave it a smart twist. It loosened slightly to the left.

"I think you've got it," Bluidy urged.

Smout turned the skull a few more revolutions exposing a hollow, inner cylinder. Inside was another piece of the map! He tapped the rolled scroll of paper into his small hand. He set down the key and smoothed the scroll flat. Smout and Bluidy nearly bumped heads as they bent excitedly over their find. The map face was nearly blank, sporting a few scant words and two short lines. The strange markings on the back were far more intriguing.

"What does it mean?" Smout asked, completely puzzled.

"I'm not entirely certain," Bluidy replied. "Wait. This clue originally led you to think of Thomas Weir, right?"

"Yes. Emma said he was Stevenson's inspiration for Henry Jekyll."

"Aha, clever girl."

"Oh, yes. She's quite bright. I always thought Stevenson had used Deacon Brodie. I suppose I was wrong."

"Why do you have to be wrong? Stevenson was influenced by many things in Edinburgh. Perhaps he used a bit of both. Maybe this clue did as well."

"What do you mean?"

"Well, perhaps your Uncle Bernie used both sources of Stevenson's inspiration for Jekyll. One to lay the false trail, and one that would lead to Brodie?"

Smout considered the possibility. He pointed to the odd markings.

"How does this lead us to Brodie?"

"Brodie was a Mason. Masons often used a secret form of writing to encode messages. This one here is called a pigpen cipher."

"Why?"

"It's easier to show you." Bluidy sketched several lines on a piece of notepaper. He filled them in with certain letters.

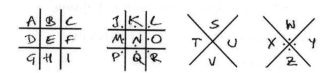

"See how the letters look a bit like pigs in pens?"

Smout nodded.

"Now, use the grids to decipher the clue."

Smout reached for the piece of paper. He matched each symbol from the map to its proper letter. When he finally finished, he sat back and read what he had written.

"A villain's wardrobe."

"There you have it!"

Smout's bow furrowed. "But what do we do with it?"

CHAPTER THIRTY-ONE

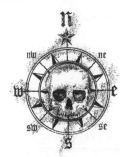

Dancing the Hempen Jig

Time was running out. No one had been able to think of a proper escape plan. Dunleavey could be back at any moment. Emma didn't even want to think about what might happen to all of them if they couldn't find a way out of their prison. She angrily tossed the loose rock she'd been fingering. It bounced off the opposite wall. She ducked instinctively as it angled back sharply and whizzed by her head. She sighed as she looked through the thick, iron bars, looking for a means of escape. There was no sign of any key that might open the heavy door of their cell. All she could see was the table, the menacing little robot with its computer, and a ballpoint pen lying uselessly on the surface.

Think, she ordered herself. What good was it being smart if you couldn't come up with a decent plan to save yourself and your friends?

Friends. The word made her smile. She looked across the cell at Bogey. The eleven-year old fished around busily in his left nostril.

Searching for inspiration, no doubt, she thought. He had a seemingly endless supply of ripe, juicy bogeys. And tongue twisters! The twister he was currently mangling was Emma's favorite by far.

"Rubber baby buggy bumpers. Rubber baby bubby bumpers. Rugger baby blubby blumpers."

Completely bizarre, Emma thought, but he was always good for a laugh.

Whispers echoing from the forward corner of the cell pulled her attention to Rory. The athletic boy conspired with Uncle Bernie. The two strategized trying to develop a plan of attack should Dunleavey come back with villainy on his mind. Bernie sketched out one possible idea in the dirt with his gnarled finger.

"As soon as he enters here," Bernie pointed to a small rock meant to represent Dunleavey, "you toss one of these rocks to knock him unconscious. A fine athlete like you, you're sure to hit your mark."

"That sounds a bit dangerous," Emma said.

"Well," Bernie replied, "unless we can figure a way out of here, I'm afraid it's the only plan we've got."

Emma watched them return to writing in the dust.

Writing! Emma had a flash of brilliance. She scurried over to Mad Dog. The large boy busied himself cracking his knuckles. Emma wasn't entirely sure, but she could have sworn he was also silently moving his lips in an attempt to master Bogey's ridiculous twisters.

They were so very different, Emma thought, she and Mad Dog. But different didn't have to mean bad. After all, it was Mad Dog's suggestion to work together that had inspired her get-away plan.

"I'm smart," Emma announced. Mad Dog froze, startled, and gave her a surly scowl. He certainly wasn't in the mood to be belittled, or get caught mumbling the silly little tongue twisters.

"Yeah. What of it?"

"Well, there are other kinds of smart. For example, I don't know how to pick a lock."

Mad Dog smiled, realizing the direction Emma's thoughts were taking. "But, I do."

"Exactly. Do you think you could pick that lock?" She pointed to the heavy iron door.

Mad Dog gave the lock a quick survey. "Yeah, I suppose I might, if I had a proper tool." All the occupants of the cell had suddenly turned their attentions to Mad Dog.

"Like what?" Emma asked hopefully, her mind on the ballpoint pen she'd seen on the table. If Rory could bounce a well-aimed rock off the wall, it might just knock the pen within reach, and Mad Dog could use it to open the lock.

"Well, it's a warded lock."

"And what tool do you need to open a warded lock?"

"A warded pick, of course."

"Of course," Emma sighed, all her brilliant hopes of using the pen lying on the table as picking tool disintegrating into dust.

"'Course, we could just try leveraging against the door and lifting it off its hinges." Mad Dog continued. "Then we wouldn't even have to worry about the lock at all." Everyone stared vacantly at Mad Dog.

"Mad Dog, you're absolutely brilliant!" Rory finally managed to stammer.

Emma stepped forward, putting her arm around Mad Dog's wide shoulders. "You're right, Rory. He is brilliant, but," she began, "his name is Maddagh."

As Smout stood on the spot, he tried not to picture what the gallows may have looked like, Burke dancing the hempen jig at the end of a thick rope, crowds cheering the man's grisly death. He was here to solve Bernie's clue.

"This is the place," he pointed to the brass markers in the ground. Fifteen metres on, the bells of St. Giles tolled sonorously. They had decided to follow the Burke and Hare clue to the spot, hoping to find something that led to the next. Smout turned in a circle, his eyes searched for a proper hiding spot for a clue. Nothing! He threw up his hands, frustrated. He felt like he'd been going in circles all day. He'd been nearly on the very same spot earlier and still felt not a bit closer to finding the treasure. The trail had gone cold.

"There's nothing here. No hiding place. No clue," Smout complained. Bluidy calmly surveyed the area. They stood on the corner where Bank met High Street. Across the way, the statue of David Hume, famous Scottish philosopher and historian, watched stoically from his position in front of the High Court building. Just up the street, Deacon Brodie's Tavern was enjoying a thriving business. Indeed, a line had formed outside the pub, full of chatty folks waiting to dine and drink under the rose and thistle ceilings.

"Maybe we're meant to go to the tavern," Bluidy suggested.

Smout shook his head. "Uncle Bernie says the tavern's only named after Brodie. I don't expect we'd find any clues there."

A glossy black cat threaded his way between Smout's legs. Smout reached down to pet the animal. As the cat began to purr, Smout let loose a wild sneeze. Startled, the cat shot off across Bank Street, nearly getting clipped by a delivery car.

"Nearly lost one of his nine lives there, I think," Bluidy chuckled.

"Nine," Smout said.

Bluidy was puzzled. "Nine? What of it?"

"Let's have a look at those the rhyme."

Smout pulled out the old 19th century skipping rhyme.

"Aha!" Smout shouted. "Look here, under the letters."

Bluidy looked where Bluidy pointing. Sure enough, there were dots under certain letters of the rhyme. Smout quickly ordered the letters in his head. His eyes widened when the solution fell into place.

"The church!" he cried.

"Yes," Bluidy responded. "The church. The next clue must be in St. Giles itself! Quick! Show me the other clue. The one I found in *St. Ives*." Smout retrieved the list of numbers Bluidy had discovered at the library.

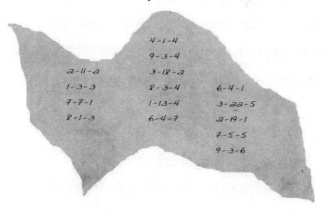

"Just as I suspected," Bluidy began. "This clue is a book cipher. See how each set of numbers falls in threes?" Smout nodded. Bluidy continued. "The first number is a line number. The second is the word."

Smout caught on, eagerly finishing the answer. "And the last number is the letter in the word."

"Spot on. Our clue must be something in the church with nine lines in it."

"The national covenant is in there," Smout offered.

"That certainly has more than nine lines. It also has nothing to do with Robert Louis Stevenson."

At that moment, a tour guide walked past them, her voice carrying that dull monotone of someone who was giving the same speech for the hundredth time. She herded her group of eager, camera-clicking tourists toward the cathedral.

"And in just a moment, we will be passing Parliament Square and entering the cathedral itself. The cathedral is a timeline, telling the history of Bonnie Scotland with a number of aisles fanning out from the four massive central pillars. Each one tells a different chapter in the story. And for those of you who like stories, please note the memorial to Robert Louis Stevenson cast by famous sculptor, Augustus Saint-Gaudens. The plaque dedicated to the famous Scots author can be found in the Moray aisle. Here we go. Watch your step."

Bluidy and Smout exchanged looks. "Well, then," Bluidy began. "Shall we take a tour?"

The pair fell in behind the group and entered the historic cathedral.

CHAPTER THIRTY-TWO

Cut & Run

It was a lucky break. At least that what Detective Inspector Markham asserted. Detective Sergeant MacGregor knew, however, that it was his attention to detail that had gotten them back on the trail of the missing boy. They could only hope to find him and the other children before Dunleavey caused them any harm.

They had followed the list of library catalogue numbers MacGregor had gotten from Bernie's offices at the museum. It had led them to the University of

Edinburgh Library where one of clerks verified seeing Smout and Bluidy just a bit earlier.

"I'm fairly certain they've gone now," she offered. "I think they were up on the third floor, though. Sorry I can't be of more help."

The policemen didn't wait for the elevator. Every second counted. They bounded up the stairs, two at a time. MacGregor was hard pressed to keep up with his superior officer. When they reached the third floor, a pimply-faced young man was collecting books from the study tables for reshelving. He pushed his cart down the aisle and was just about to grab the books Smout and Bluidy had reviewed when Markham shouted.

"Stop! Police!"

The young man froze, nervously raising his hands in the air. "I'm sorry, officer. Whatever it is, I promise I didn't do it," he squeaked.

"Oh, put your hands down. We just need to see those books."

The young man sighed in relief. Markham flipped through the books already on the young man's cart, searching for something that might give a clue to Smout's next destination. MacGregor sat in the chair and looked at the titles on the table.

"Here we go," he said, pointing to the catalogue numbers typed on the spines. "These are the ones. They're both on the list."

MacGregor and Markham compared the numbers to those in MacGregor's notes. They turned slowly as they realized the young man was also studying the numbers right over their shoulders.

"If you will excuse us, this is a police investigation," Markham growled.

"Sorry to intrude. I was just curious." The young man scratched at an angry, red pimple on his chin. "Is this one of them cold cases?"

One fuzzy eyebrow lifted over Markham's curious stare. "Why do you say that?"

"Oh, it's just I've been reshelving these books for a while now. I practically know the numbers by heart. Nearly all the books on that list are stories written by Robert Louis Stevenson and everybody knows he's long since dead. Say," the young man began, heartened by the prospect of excitement in his otherwise dull day. "You don't suppose he was secretly murdered, do you, and that's why you're investigating?"

"No. We don't believe Stevenson was murdered."

"Oh." The young man's face fell. "Shame really. Now that's a story Stevenson would have liked to write himself."

"You said *all* these books were written by Stevenson?" MacGregor asked certain now that the pattern had something to do with their case.

"Except that one," the young man continued. He pointed to *The Oxford Nursery Rhyme Book.* The policeman's face fell. He truly thought he'd been onto something.

"May I go now?" the young man asked. Markham nodded.

He gathered the two books from the policemen and placed them on his cart. "It is curious, though," he began. "Both these books *do* have something to with St. Ives."

319

The two men popped to attention. They rushed to the young man's side. "St. Ives? What of it?"

Flustered, the young man searched for words. "Yes, um, St. Ives. *St. Ives* was a book Stevenson wrote."

"What was it about?" Markham demanded, crushing the young man's lapels in his big hands.

"A prisoner! A French prisoner!"

A prisoner?

"Sir?" MacGregor asked.

"What?"

"This treasure hunt Dunleavey mentioned?"

"Yes? What of it?"

MacGregor tapped his notepad with his pen. "Well, suppose there's something to it. What if all these titles are clues? Clues that lead to this supposed treasure."

"And if we follow the trail, we might just find our missing archaeologist and the children."

"Exactly right, sir."

Markham grabbed the librarian's assistant

MELINDA TALIANCICH FALGOUST

firmly by the shoulders. "The prisoner! In the book, where was the prisoner held?"

"At the Castle, of course. At Edinburgh Castle."

The two policemen rushed toward the stairs, causing a dervish of notepapers to spin off the nearby table. The flustered young man knelt to retrieve them, his heart rate pulsing rapidly. The life of a librarian's assistant was so exciting!

The loose gravel cracked like gunfire under the screeching tires of Dunleavey's car as it skidded to a stop in the Holyrood car park. He was in no mood for delay. The children knew the real location of the treasure and they would confess the information to him. No more wild goose chases.

He knew how to deal with children. Spare the rod and spoil the child indeed. They simply needed the proper persuasion. Perhaps, Dunleavey thought as he and Sandoval made quick work of the path to the hidden tunnel entrance, he would finally be able to make use of Sandoval's robot. The expensive piece of junk certainly hadn't provided any assistance in finding the treasure. He thought of the sharp hook on the end of the invention's long, probing arm. Yes, he thought. Perhaps the threat of a little blood might loosen their little tongues. He smiled evilly as he and Sandoval vanished into the side of the mountain.

Sweat ran in rivulets down the children's faces. The five of them, the four mismatched children and one bedraggled adult, leveraged themselves against the door, straining to provide enough upward pressure to lift the door free from its hinges. The ancient door began to groan, giving them incentive to push harder.

"Put your backs into it," Maddagh ordered. They gave a mighty shove and the door lifted several inches. It tottered precariously for a brief moment then clamored with an echoing clang on the stone floor.

Rory stood in slack-jawed amazement. "I can't believe that actually worked."

Maddagh dusted his hands on his pants.

"Simple lever fulcrum principle, really." He

stared at the flabbergasted faces. "What? So, I watch a lot of *Mythbusters* on the Beeb."

"Maddagh, you're absolutely amazing," Emma blurted. Maddagh blushed.

Their ears still rang from the echoing crash, so it took a few moments before they heard the voices. Bogey was the first to react.

"What's that?"

The rest of the group listened intently. One by one, they all heard the angry cries coming from the hidden tunnel.

Dunleavey was back.

And he didn't sound happy.

Certainly, he had heard the noise from their escape attempt. Rory grabbed Emma's sleeve.

"Let's go!"

He didn't need to make the suggestion twice. They ran.

He felt flushed. At first, he supposed he was nervous, nervous that so many people were counting on him. His uncle. His friends. If he didn't succeed in finding the treasure, who knew what Dunleavey might do. How did he, the small and wimpy kid who got stuffed into lockers, ever expect to find a treasure that had managed to stay hidden for centuries? He wasn't some great, larger-than-life adventurer like his uncle. Or even Mr. Bluidy, for that matter.

But Smout began to realize the real reason for the fever that was creeping into his cheeks – he was enjoying this treasure hunt. For the first time since the disappearance of his mother, Smout was enjoying himself. He had left the safe and boring confines of Uncle Bernie's flat and, weak lungs or not, had really begun to breathe. He was enjoying the adventure of discovering his own city, Stevenson's city, as he followed the mysterious clues across Edinburgh. He couldn't wait to get to the next one.

So, as he stood before the Saint-Gauden's plaque inside the cathedral, his fevered brain worked frantically at puzzling out Bernie's next hint. The cipher.

The memorial was a low-relief plaque, cast in bronze. A border of ivy leaves and berries framed the famous author, reclined on a chaise, pen held aloft in a moment of creative thought. It was lovely, to be sure, but what interested Smout was the poetry neatly engraved in nine, straight lines

.

Give us grace and strength to forebear and preserve. Give us courage and gaiety and the quiet mind, spare to us our friends, soften us to our enemies, bless us, if it may be, in all our innocent endeavors. If it may not, give us the strength to encounter that which is to come, that we may be brave in peril, constant in tribulation,

temperate in wrath,

and in all changes of fortune,

and down to the gates of death,

loyal and loving

to one another.

Smout used the cipher, matching each trio of numbers in the code to its corresponding letter. Suddenly, he looked up at Bluidy.

"I know where we have to go."

Dunleavey stood over the useless cell door and stared into the empty alcove where Bernie and the children had been imprisoned just moments ago. His face reddened like a boiled lobster. He let loose a bellow that rocked the foundations of the Castle itself.

"No!"

He gripped the sides of the small robot and

325

shattered it to the ground, its probing hook snapping off, a useless appendage. Sandoval shrieked in agony.

"You monster!" he cried, falling to the ground next to his beloved invention.

Dunleavey leaned in close to Sandoval's doughy face.

"Monster? You haven't even begun to see the monster I can be. Find the old man and the children, now, before they reach the topside of the Castle, or your precious little robot will not be the only thing in little bitty pieces." His voice rumbled just below a whisper, but the threat carried a morbid promise.

Sandoval scrambled to his feet and loped off into another darkened corridor. Dunleavey watched as his hitching gait was swallowed by the blackness.

CHAPTER THIRTY- THREE

Sea Change

Smout and Bluidy burst into the purpling twilight. The last pink fingers of daylight groped across the evening sky. Soon it would be dark. Dangerous things happened in the dark, Smout thought. Everyone knew that's when the monsters came out. And his friends were being held hostage by one of the worst.

The sobering thought put a speed in his step. He scrambled up High Street towards Bank, but at the corner skidded to a sudden stop. Bluidy nearly

327

trammeled right over him.

"What is it?"

Smout pointed to the car trying to edge its way through a particularly large group of pedestrians crossing the street.

"Detective Inspector Markham!"

Sure enough, the policeman's car was just coming across the George IV Bridge headed for the Castle. Smout tried to duck out of sight, but the Inspector had already seen him. Markham nearly tossed MacGregor from the car, pointing furiously through the windscreen in Smout's direction. Finally, MacGregor spied him as well and began to give chase. There wasn't much time.

Smout's hand found the map pieces in his pocket. He had found nearly every piece. The map was almost complete. He was sure if he followed this last clue, it would finally lead him to the treasure. If he got pinched now, his chance was blown. There was only one thing left to do.

"Take the map!" he urged Bluidy. He shoved all six pieces into Bluidy's hand. "They haven't seen

MELINDA TALIANCICH FALGOUST

you. They don't know you're with me. If you leave now, you have a chance to find the treasure and help me get Uncle Bernie and the others back."

Bluidy couldn't believe his ears. The boy was willingly giving him the map. Faint stirrings of guilt began to churn in his gut. He looked into the boy's eyes, Victoria's eyes.

"Please!" Smout begged. "You're all I've got."

Bluidy decided. He closed his fist around the fragments of map. "I'll do it."

Relief washed over Smout. He let go a heavy sigh. "Use the last few clues. Find the treasure. We'll use it to trade for Uncle Bernie and my friends. We'll need to contact Mr. Dunleavey, somehow. To set up the exchange."

"Oh, don't worry about Dunleavey. When you want something as badly as he does, he'll find you."

"Okay, then. We'll need to pick a place for the trade."

"Someplace public," Bluidy agreed.

329

A stray firework, no doubt a precursor of the night's festivities, arced over the Castle, and erupted in a shower of cherry red sparks. Bluidy and Smout looked at each other.

"The Castle!" they voiced simultaneously.

The exploding pyrotechnics had momentarily distracted MacGregor. He, along with the wandering pedestrians "oohing" and "aahing", stared almost instinctively at the quickly dissipating sparks. It was just enough time for Bluidy to sneak away.

"I'll explain things to the Inspector. Now, go!" Smout urged.

Bluidy limped quickly away, melting into the crowd. Smout took a deep breath. "Well, here goes."

He stepped out in full view of Sergeant MacGregor. MacGregor snagged him by the elbow.

"Gotcha! We've been looking for you, young man. You've got a lot of explaining to do, but it will have to wait. We think we know where your uncle might be, but there's no time to lose."

The Inspector pulled up alongside. He opened the door and waved them inside. "Come on, then!

Step lively!" Smout and Sergeant MacGregor piled into the Inspector's car.

Just up the street, hidden round the corner of the High Court building, Bluidy watched them pull away. As soon as they melted into the clog of traffic, Bluidy looked down at the cipher's solution Smout had scribbled on the back of the section of map. Lady Stair's Close.

Bluidy smiled. The boy was smart. He had to give him that. Lady Stair's Close was home to Edinburgh's Writers' Museum. The museum housed a number of artifacts from many of Scotland's most famous authors – Robert Burns, Sir Walter Scott, and, of course, Robert Louis Stevenson. With any amount of luck, Bluidy thought, it also housed the final clue to the treasure. Then perhaps he could put Edinburgh and all its memories behind him for good. He pocketed the map and began the upward walk to the close.

With no torch to guide their way, the children kept stumbling as they made their way up the slippery steps toward escape. Bogey tripped into Maddagh for the hundredth time.

"Oof! Sorry," Bogey apologized. "I can't see a thing." He felt his way along the slimy dampness. He cringed. It felt like a massive wall of bogeys. Maybe he needed to rethink his unusual hobby.

"Where does this even lead, anyhow?" he asked.

"Who cares as long as it's away from that lunatic Dunleavey," Maddagh shadowy figure cracked.

"Keep heading upward," Bernie voice urged. "If I'm correct, the dungeon we were being held in is below the regular Castle vaults where they hold the Prisoners of War Exhibition. Keep going and we should muddle our way out to Crown Square."

"Will there be guards?" Bogey warbled, the darkness failing to hide the pitchy nervousness in his voice.

"Yes, I suppose there should be. Especially with the start of the Tattoo on us."

"Good," Bogey said. "Because the bad guys

are right behind us! Run!"

Sure enough, the group could hear a labored snuffling sound behind them. The jogging oblong spot of a torch beam played on the walls of the staircase. The chase was on.

The slow, careful ascent through the dark suddenly became a headlong rush filled with dangerous sliding. If one of them managed to slip and crack their head on the unforgiving stone, it would mean certain capture. Or worse.

The heavy breathing echoing behind them only seemed to be getting closer.

"Faster!" Rory urged.

Suddenly, a hand clutched at Bogey's arm.

"I have you now, *mi pequeño conejo*," Sandoval growled. His hot breath brushed the nape of Bogey's neck. The light from his torch cast disfiguring shadows on his face, altering his already doughy face into a ghoulish nightmare.

Bogey screamed.

"Bogey!" the group cried collectively.

Maddagh was the first to rush to his

assistance. Beefy fists landed on Sandoval. The Spaniard lost his grip on the torch and it clattered to the steps. It spun wildly, creating dancing shadows on the wall as Maddagh, then Rory and Uncle Bernie, tried to wrest Bogey from the man's grasp. It was difficult for any of them to gain purchase in the slippery, narrow space.

"We want the treasure!" Sandoval demanded, refusing to release Bogey from his grasp. In a last, desperate maneuver, Sandoval yanked Bogey to him, one arm tightening around the boy like a vise.

"Step back!" Sandoval warned. "One false move and I will throw your friend down this staircase."

Bernie and the children stepped back. Bernie looked at the worried faces of the children and decided. He took one step closer to Sandoval.

"Very well," Bernie began. "You have given me no choice."

The children, Bogey included, immediately cast troubled looks at Bernie. They had come too far to give up on the treasure now.

"I can't let you harm the boy. No treasure is worth that."

Sandoval grinned, his gold tooth glinting in the uncertain light of the torch. "Good. I'm glad we understand each other."

Emma, whose hand had been gripping Rory's arm, suddenly squeezed the boy so tightly he winced.

"What?" Rory whispered.

"I have a plan," she whispered back. Rory gave her a puzzled look. She touched her finger to her nose then pointed at Bogey. Rory suddenly realized what she was getting at. Rory caught Maddagh's eye. Maddagh watched as Rory touched his nose and pointed at Bogey. Maddagh nodded almost imperceptibly. He looked at Bogey, still trapped in Sandoval's vise-like grip.

"I'll give you the location of the treasure if you'll just let the boy go," Bernie offered.

"A reasonable trade," Sandoval began.

At that moment, however, Maddagh caught Bogey's attention. He touched his nose and pointed at Sandoval. Bogey immediately understood.

335

He took his free hand, pointed his finger straight up into the air, and dove in deep. While Sandoval negotiated with Uncle Bernie, Bogey fished around his nasal passages for the ripest, greenest, stickiest bogey he had ever found.

The rest of the group watched as a broad smile spread across Bogey's small face. He'd found one!

He pulled his finger free and smeared the gob of green mucus across Sandoval's arm. Sandoval shrieked in disgust and immediately released Bogey in a vain attempt to wipe the offending slime away.

"Run!" Bogey bellowed, snatching up Sandoval's torch and plowing forward.

"That was excellent!" Maddagh huffed appreciatively between breaths as they rushed up the stairs.

"Not everyone may appreciate my art," Bogey gasped as he ran, "but it certainly has a way of sticking with people."

The children's laughter echoed off the stone walls and down to Sandoval who flailed uselessly in the dark, desperately trying to wipe away Bogey's bogey.

CHAPTER THIRTY-FOUR

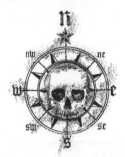

X Marks the Spot

Sarah Knox turned the key in the lock. Out of habit, she tugged firmly on the door handle, checking that all was secure. She had made certain that everything had been properly dusted, straightened, and that any crumbs fallen from contraband crisps smuggled into the museum were neatly swept away. Couldn't have any uninvited rodent chewing at Stevenson's fishing basket or leaving nasty little droppings on Sir Walter Scott's printing press. It was her job as curator to ensure the safety of all these historical items and preserve them for generations to come.

Satisfied the door was quite secure, she dropped her keys in her purse and turned. She let loose a little gasp when she nearly bumped into Bluidy, who stood quietly in the shadows.

"Oh, my goodness!" she fluttered, clutching her hand to he chest. "Pardon me. I'm sorry, sir, but the museum is closed for the day. You're certainly welcome to come back in the morning. We reopen promptly at 10:00 a.m.".

Bluidy stepped forward, leaning heavily on his cane. "Forgive me if I startled you, Miss. I understand the museum is closed, but I'm afraid I must ask if you would allow me inside for just a brief moment."

Sara eyed Bluidy warily. No one else was in the courtyard. If he tried anything funny, she was completely on her own. She reached a hand into her bag, fingers searching for her pepper spray.

Bluidy sensed her unease. He had to get into that museum and find the next clue. Tonight. He was so close to the treasure, he could taste it. This would require a little finesse. He smiled broadly.

"It's my son, you see. We were here earlier." Bluidy offered the lie with practiced ease. "He thinks he left something inside the museum."

"Left something?" Sara asked, her anxiety giving way to irritation. If this was over some bleeping, beeping video game.

"Yes," Bluidy answered, taking a step forward. He carefully measured his next statement. "It's just a book, a dog-eared copy of *Treasure Island*. Stevenson is one of his favorite authors, you see. That's why we came here. To the museum."

"Of course," Sara offered a benevolent smile. She was always glad to meet a fellow admirer of the great author.

"Well, I realize what an imposition this is, but his mother gave it to him, you see." Bluidy bowed his head sadly. "I'm afraid she's gone now."

Sara was sold. She stepped forward, patting Bluidy's arm affectionately. "Oh, the poor lamb. I completely understand. Say no more. I suppose a quick look around couldn't hurt. For the boy."

Sara turned to unlock the door.

Bluidy smiled even wider. "Yes. Of course. For the boy."

Detective Inspector Markham, Detective Sergeant MacGregor, and Smout weaved their way through the tightly packed queue forming near the Castle Esplanade. The people bubbled with excitement. If the welling crowd was any indication, the Tattoo was an event not to be missed.

They were not here for the entertainment. The Inspector flashed his identification at the entrance and was waved through. Once inside the gate, the trio was overwhelmed by the sheer enormity of it all. Steep bleacher seating bordered three sides of the Esplanade, seating that was already burgeoning with an expectant audience.

Markham waved his hands in the air. "Where are we supposed to find them in all this?" he blustered. A large, boisterous group of American college lads shouldered past.

"Blasted tourist season," Markham growled. "It's a wonder there's even anyone left on the other side of the pond!"

"The vaults!" MacGregor yelled over the building buzz of the crowd.

They scurried down the steps to the show area, where Markham had to show his credentials once again. He quickly muttered something into the large guard's ear. The guard quickly grabbed several coworkers, and the group of men began a quick sprint across the expanse of the Esplanade. Smout made a start to follow on their heels, but MacGregor put out a halting hand.

"Oh, no. Where do you think you're going?"

"With you, of course."

"Not likely." MacGregor smiled. He knelt on one knee so his face was at Smout's level and gently held the boy by the shoulders. "Listen, son. You've done a bang-up job getting this far, but now it's time for you to step aside and let us do our job."

Smout snorted. "Where have I heard that before?"

"You can like it or not, but there's no way you're coming down into those vaults with us." MacGregor stood and steered Smout toward a friendly-looking female officer nearby. "You are going to stay put right here while we wrap this thing up. Then, quick as a wink, before you can say Bob's your uncle, we'll have you back with your friends and family and this whole nasty business will be behind us."

MacGregor took a few steps away then turned back. "Maybe try and enjoy a bit of the Tattoo." The policeman took off at a jog.

"Sure," Smout muttered *sotto voce*. "You've done spectacularly so far."

Then, as an afterthought, he sucked in a lungful of courage and shouted after the policeman.

"And my uncle's name isn't Bob! It's Bernie!"

"Where do suppose your boy left it?" Sara called out to Bluidy as she went about turning on the lights in the museum. Bluidy, of course, paid her no heed. He was too busy searching.

Bernie had been clever about the clues, especially this one. His brother certainly hadn't wanted to make finding the treasure easy for just anyone. Bluidy had to admit, Smout had been quite clever to follow his brother's twisting trail through the city as far as he had. But it wasn't truly twisting, now was it?

No, another distinct pattern had emerged from the locations hinted at by Bernie's clues. Four cleverly placed locations around the city.

Bluidy had nearly missed the clue hidden in *St. Ives*. Yes, the novel was set at Edinburgh Castle, and that was important, but his brother's clue had also sent them specifically to page one where the chapter title blazed – *Tale of a Lion Rampant*. Bluidy wondered how many people knew the Scottish Royal Banner of Arms by that name. There were only a few places in Scotland where it was permitted to fly, and Holyrood Palace enjoyed that honor. Now, as he stood in the fifth location, in front of the Brodie wardrobe once owned by Robert Louis Stevenson, he connected the dots in his head. Very clever, Bernie, Bluidy smiled. He wondered if the children would have beaten him to the treasure if left to their own designs.

It didn't matter now. Bernie had disappeared, Smout was in police custody, and he, Jack Bluidy, stood here on the verge of finding the treasure. He looked up at the wardrobe. No, he corrected himself – a villain's wardrobe.

"I think we took a wrong turn down in those tunnels," Bogey gasped as Bernie and the fleeing children tumbled into the artificial daylight of the Crown Square. "I think we're in India."

Blinking against the sudden contrast between the dark vaults and the intensity of the lights in the staging area, the small group found themselves in the midst of a gathering cluster of *gurkhas*. The burnished ochre of their skin and menacing *kukri*, long, sword-like knives curving at their sides, did lend a certain other-wordly feel to the current surroundings. Of course, the *gurkhas* were equally as confused at the sudden appearance of four young children and a ragged old man.

Bernie quickly stepped forward. "No, no, no, my young friends. We are not in India. These are *gurkhas*, Nepalese warriors. They are here for the Tattoo. Mind the *kukri*, if you please."

"*Kukris*?" Maddagh asked, confused. "I thought you said they were *gurkhas*." It was much more education than Maddagh was willing to absorb in one day.

"The knives, my dear boy. Curious custom the *gurkhas* have about the *kukri*," Bernie babbled. Maddagh yanked his sleeve and pulled the man forward.

"I'm not sure now is the best time for a history lesson, Mr. McManus."

"At least now I know where Smout gets it," Rory replied.

"We'd better get moving," Bogey suggested, a nervous tremor shaking his voice. "Those nasty characters are still after us, you know." They quickly began to thread their way through the mass of performers.

Sandoval was, indeed, still in pursuit. They couldn't guarantee the congested square would deter him from trying to recapture them. And no one was certain where Dunleavey had gone. He could be lurking anywhere.

CHAPTER THIRTY-FIVE

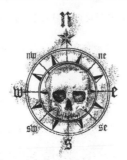

Captain Smout

Smout could stand it no longer. He'd been sitting there for a full fifteen minutes, eyes glued to the stone arch of the Castle entrance, but there had been no sign of the Inspector, his uncle, or his friends. What he did see, however, was a suspiciously familiar figure slinking under the portcullis gate. Dunleavey!

Smout waited until the female officer looked away and ran.

Emma wanted nothing more than to run – run

and put this whole crazy adventure behind her. But the crowd was too thick. Turtles moved with greater speed. Emma looked around nervously for the rest of the group. She thought she spied the back of Rory's sandy-brown head bobbing along in the sea of people, but she couldn't be sure. Soon it was hopelessly apparent. She had fallen behind.

"Rory!" she called, but the young man couldn't hear her. The mechanical growl of a motorcycle engine on her right caused her to jump. A member of the Imps Motorcycle Display Team was simply testing his engine. Emma sighed in relief.

Someone suddenly gripped her arm like a vise. Emma yelped. When she spied the sporran and familiar tartan of the pipe and drum corps, her fears began to subside. It was just one of the pipers, she thought. Then she looked up and saw the livid face of the malicious Mr. Dunleavey.

"Now, let's go get your friends, shall we?" he sneered, and pushed her roughly through the crowd.

He had to be quick. The curator would be

back at any moment. Bluidy opened the upper doors of the wardrobe. He searched each crack and crevice, looking for something Bernie had left behind. Nothing.

He pulled open the lower drawers. There it was. Wedged in one of the seams was a torn scrap. Quickly, but gently, Bluidy worked it free. The footsteps of the curator echoed from down the hall. Bluidy hastily shut the doors and drawers of the wardrobe. He had just finished when Miss Knox returned.

"Did you find what you were looking for?" she asked sweetly.

Bluidy smiled winningly and patted his pocket. "Yes, Miss. Yes, I did."

The Inspector scanned the thick crowd of performers, searching for any sign of the missing children and the archaeologist.

"There they are!" MacGregor cried. He pointed to the cluster making its way through the throng. "And McManus is with them! Kids! Over here!"

The children spied the welcome sight of MacGregor's familiar face. They were safe!

"Never thought I'd be glad to see the cops," Maddagh chuckled. Uncle Bernie cast a dubious look his way.

"Nevermind," Maddagh offered. "Long story."

"We're just glad you're all alright," MacGregor stated as he shook Bernie's hand. "We'll want to take your statements, of course, but we'll get to that. Let's just get all of you back to your families, right?" There were hearty head nods all around.

"Well, I'll be," Markham mumbled. The Inspector was overwhelmed with relief at the sight of the children. He ran his hand through his wild hair, scratching his head in puzzlement. How did three children manage to locate a missing person that seasoned veteran police officers had failed to find?

Wait, Markham thought. Three children? Markham worked it out in his head. Young Smout was out in the stands. That should have left four children unaccounted for. Markham immediately counted heads. No, there were definitely only three children present. Markham interrupted the premature celebration.

"Where is Miss Johnson?" he asked.

Everyone looked around, expecting to see Emma with another of their group, but she was nowhere to be seen.

"Where is she?" Rory worried.

"I thought she was with you," Maddagh countered. Rory shook his head.

"Is this what you're looking for?" A familiar voice parted the crowd. The police, the performers, Bernie, and the children all turned in the direction of the voice. There stood Dunleavey, in full Highland piper garb, holding a dirk to Emma's throat. The police instinctively surged forward to rescue her, but Dunleavey pushed the point of the knife into her skin.

"Ah, ah, ah," he warned, wagging a cautionary finger. "Stand back! We wouldn't want Miss Johnson to miss her classes tomorrow, now would we?" No one dared move.

"Dunleavey, don't you dare harm a hair on that girl's head," Markham threatened.

"Well, now, that depends entirely on Mr. McManus there." Dunleavey gave a quick gesture to Bernie. "I'll make this quite simple. Where's the treasure, Bernard?"

Markham's fuzzy eyebrows popped up in surprise. He couldn't quite believe what his ears were hearing. "You mean there really is a treasure?" he whispered. "I thought it was all poppycock."

"Does it really matter?" Bernie asked. "He believes it's real and now because of it, Miss Johnson is in very real danger." He stood as tall as his five-foot-six frame would allow. "I can't allow her to come to any harm. I have to tell him where it is."

Emma squirmed in Dunleavey's grasp. "No, Mr. McManus. You can't!"

"No!" Rory and the others rushed forward, but MacGregor and the Castle security guards held them back.

Rory turned to Maddagh. "There's got to be something we can do. Sneak up behind him perhaps?"

The big boy shrugged. "And do what?"

Rory looked up at Dunleavey. He calculated the variables. The dastardly villain gripped one arm wrapped tightly around Emma, but the hand with the knife struggled to keep the weapon at Emma's throat. He kept tugging at the kilt which promised to slide right off his narrow hips. Perhaps? A kernel of an idea began to germinate then withered almost as quickly. Rory's shoulders sank.

"I have no idea," Rory said.

Everyone's eyes were locked onto the harrowing scene unfolding before them. No one noticed the *kukri* blade being slipped from its sheath. Certainly not the *gurkha* to whom it belonged. The thief skirted round the edges of the crowd with his newly acquired weapon.

Bernie squared his shoulders. He looked directly at Dunleavey. "Before I give up the treasure's location, I want some assurances from you."

Dunleavey laughed. "Oh, I don't think you in

any position to ask for anything, now are you." It would have sounded more threatening, but the kilt began to creep southward again. As it was, Dunleavey grabbed the slipping garment, quickly readjusting the knife to a position in dangerous proximity to Emma's carotid artery.

Position was exactly what was on Smout's mind. The hand holding the *kukri* blade began to sweat. He gripped the hardwood handle even tighter. He tiptoed from the periphery of the growing crowd, edging along the wall that bordered the ledge where Dunleavey stood. The hand that held the *kukri* blade began to sweat. He gripped the hardwood handle even tighter.

His furtive movements caught Bogey's eye. Bogey tugged rapidly on Rory's sleeve. He nodded discreetly toward the ledge where Dunleavey stood. Rory and Maddagh followed his gaze. Smout slid along the wall behind Dunleavey, sticking closely to the shadows.

Bernie spied his nephew and quickly looked back at Dunleavey.

"Very well. I suppose you leave me no choice. The treasure is -". The revelation hung in the air. An almost a tangible surge rippled through the crowd as almost everyone gathered in the square leaned forward.

At that moment, Smout leapt from the shadows, wielding the *kukri* with an expertise earned from all the mock battles he had played at with Uncle Bernie in their living room. He skillfully sliced through the two leather straps securing Dunleavey's kilt. He grabbed Emma and spun clear as the bright green tartan fell to the ground. The surprise attack yielded the desired effect.

Dunleavey's pale white legs and knobby knees were quite exposed as he suddenly stood there in nothing but his knickers. Instinctively, he dropped the dirk and clutched awkwardly for the lost kilt. It gave the police the distraction they needed to rush forward and apprehend the red-faced Dunleavey.

"At least he wasn't wearing it regimental," Markham said as they slapped the handcuffs on the skinny secretary. MacGregor nodded in hearty agreement.

Bernie and the boys rejoined Emma and Smout. Hearty handshakes and hugs were exchanged all around. Bogey blathered effusely about Maddagh's mad science skills that had helped them escape.

"It weren't nothing, really," Maddagh replied. He clapped Smout on the back, knocking his glasses sideways. "Now, Smout's move was pure dead brilliant! I couldn't have done it better myself!" Maddagh said.

"Yeah, well, you were sort of my inspiration," Smout replied. He reached up to straighten his glasses.

Maddagh lowered his head sheepishly. "Yeah. About that. I'm, uh, really sorry about all the times I pantsed you."

"And stuffed him in the locker," Rory added.

"And gave him swirlies in the loo," Bogey interjected.

"And stole his lunch money," Emma included.

Maddagh threw his hands in the air. "Alright!

I get the picture! Anyway, it wasn't very sporting of me, was it?"

They all nodded in agreement. Maddagh grabbed Smout round the shoulders and pulled him close. "I guess what I'm trying to say is, for a swot, you're alright."

Smout grinned. He punched Maddagh playfully in the arm. "And for a boffin, you make a pretty good friend. You all do."

"Yeah?" Maddagh asked, surprise in his tone.

The children all looked at each other and agreed.

"Yeah," they replied in unison.

Bernie smiled from ear to ear. He put his arms round the children's shoulders. "What a fabulous adventure! Now, what do you say we all go watch the opening festivities of the Tattoo?"

The children looked at Bernie as if he had thoroughly gone round the bend.

"But, Uncle Bernie." Smout looked around to see if anyone was listening. "What about the treasure?"

"Yes," Bernie replied. "What about the treasure?"

"I've given Bluidy all the clues."

"Bluidy?" Bogey suddenly remembered Rory's revelation regarding the mysterious man. "Smout!"

Rory clapped his hand over Bogey's mouth. It wasn't the right time to share what they had discovered. Rory whispered in Bogey's ear. "Not now."

Bogey nodded.

"You've given him all the clues, you say?" Uncle Bernie asked.

"Yes. He's been helping all along." Smout turned to the others. "He was saving me from Dunleavey back at the train station. Not trying to hurt me. He was helping me find the treasure's location. We were going to use the information to bargain with Mr. Dunleavey. He was supposed to meet me here at the Castle."

"Was he, now?" Bernie scratched his beard. He spent a long moment lost in thought, then clapped his hands together. "Then if Mr. Bluidy is clever enough to discover the treasure's true location, perhaps he will."

"The treasure's *true* location?" Emma asked. "What's that supposed to mean?"

"Aha! That, my dear, is the real riddle, isn't it?"

"No," interrupted Detective Inspector Markham. He walked up to the group steering a very sullen Dunleavey. "The real riddle is how the lot of you managed to get into so much trouble. And I expect we haven't seen the last of it, have we?"

The members of the ragtag group exchanged knowing glances.

"Yeah, I suppose I can see me hanging around with this sorry lot," Maddagh said. "They're probably going to need a little muscle around. Someone with a bit of street smarts and scientific know-how."

"And I suppose they're going to need somebody who knows the difference between a *cretin* and a Croatian. They might misread a map and get dreadfully lost. So, I'll stick around, too, I suppose," Emma said.

"And you never know if a good puzzle will need solving, so I'm in," Rory said.

"Or when the expert skills of an escape artist like me will be needed," Bogey suggested.

"Humph!" Markham huffed. "And who's the captain of this little crew?"

Without hesitation, the children all shouted in chorus.

"Smout!"

Smout blinked in disbelief. Him? Captain? Uncle Bernie wrapped his arm around him. "Why not?"

Smout slowly smiled. "Yo ho ho?"

The entire gang erupted in a happy cheer.

"Well, I suppose I'm going to have to keep a wary eye on you five. Try not to get into too much trouble, and that goes for you as well, Mr. McManus."

The Inspector pointed to Uncle Bernie. "Can I expect you'll forget about this ridiculous treasure hunt in favor of safer activities?"

"No guarantees, Inspector. I am, after all, a McManus. But, for now, at least, I plan to stay close to home."

"See that you do. Very well, then. As for you," the Inspector narrowed a stern gaze at the felonious secretary. "We'll see to it that you're put away somewhere where you can't bother these kids."

"This isn't over, McManus," Dunleavey muttered. "I'll be back. You just wait. And maybe next time you won't have one of those fancy knives."

Smout realized he still had the *kukri.* "Did you know that the *gurkhas* have a legend about the *kukri*?"

Rory rolled his eyes. "Here we go again!"

"No, it's true! Once the *kukri* had been drawn, it cannot be resheathed until it's tasted blood!" He brandished the weapon wildly in the air. Suddenly, it slipped from his sweaty grip and landed, sharp point down, right on Dunleavey's big toe.

"Yow!" Dunleavey howled, hopping awkwardly with his hands cuffed behind his back.

"Mission accomplished!" Bogey giggled.

The Inspector shook his head. He retrieved the blade and escorted his limping prisoner away.

Meanwhile, Detective Sergeant MacGregor handed off a squirming Sandoval to Castle security. They had found the Spaniard skulking through the dark corridors of the Castle vaults, fumbling for an exit. He seemed only too happy to turn Crown's evidence on Dunleavey.

"He destroyed my little *Piratino*!" he spat.

MacGregor turned to the children. "Well, you're certainly a smart bunch. Following all those clues. Who knows? You might have a future on the force."

"I might not have figured it out if weren't for your notepad, Sergeant," Smout confessed. "I saw the list of library numbers on your desk."

"Yes," the Sergeant agreed. "Sometimes the little things are the most important." He pulled out his notepad and handed it to Smout. "Here. Take this. Write down everything that makes you wonder, no matter how trivial you think it might be. You

363

never know what small detail might hold the answer."

Smout smiled wide in appreciation. He took the small book from the policeman. He flipped through the pages, pausing on the one that held the comical sketch of Detective Inspector Markham. Smout looked up at MacGregor curiously. The young man hurriedly urged him to close the book.

"We'll just keep that between you and me, alright?"

Smout grinned.

An officer stepped up with the dangling ruins of Sandoval's robot.

"What shall I do with this, sir?"

Maddagh cleared his throat. "Would it be alright if I could have it? I think I can fix it. I'd like to give it a go, at any rate."

MacGregor smiled. "Why not? Might keep you out of trouble. For a spot, anyway."

Maddagh gratefully took the pile of broken mechanics from the policeman.

"By the by, wherever did Mr. Bluidy get off to? You kids had quite a story to tell about him back at the station," MacGregor continued.

"It was all a misunderstanding, Sergeant," Smout burst before anyone else could get in a word. "Mr. Bluidy actually helped us get away from Mr. Dunleavey. I'm not really sure where he is now."

"Well, I hope we find him. I'd like to thank him for keeping you kids safe from harm. I should be off, now. Cheerio!" MacGregor gave a wave and walked toward the exit.

"I do wonder where Bluidy is," Rory asked as the strange, ragtag bunch moved toward the viewing area.

"Me, too," Smout replied. "Me, too." *That* was a burning riddle Smout desperately wanted to solve.

CHAPTER THIRTY-SIX

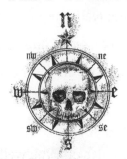

The Gubbins Club

The riddle sat innocuously on the table. It lay next to the letter with which it had arrived. Solve me, it taunted.

The answer is hidden among the stars.

.Smout just stared blankly at both items. Everyone else in the room just stared at him.

The envelope was postmarked from London, England, addressed to Master Colin McManus. The letter was from Bluidy.

No, Smout corrected himself. It was from his father. Smout picked up the letter and reread it.

Dearest Colin-

I hope this letter find you well, though I have no reason to believe you are otherwise. You're a smart boy. Very much like your mother. Which brings me to the reason for this correspondence. When I said your mother and I were partners, I was not lying. I was also I'm afraid, not entirely truthful. She was my wife, Colin, which I'm sure if you're the intelligent young man I believe you to be, you will have realized makes me your father. I did not perish on an

367

archaeological excursion as your mother and uncle may have told you. Rather, I left the two of you to seek greater fortunes elsewhere. I changed my name, my appearance, and went off in search of gold. Sadly, I realize now that the two of you were the greatest treasure any man could possibly hope for and I fear with this confession, I may lose you forever. I don't know how my brother found me. Of course, treasure hunting runs in the family blood, so perhaps I should not be surprised at all. I can only thank him for helping me realize what I should truly be searching for. I solved his puzzle. I found the treasure. But, I leave the adventure to you, my son, and have enclosed the clue with this letter. Stevenson was correct. No man is lonely that has a friend, and you have found four loyal companions.

They will look after you on your
adventures while I embark on my own.
I am off to find your mother. If she is
alive, and I pray she is, I will use every
resource in my power to bring her back
to you. Perhaps if I succeed, you
might both forgive me and we can,
once again, be a family.

Yours,

Duncan Archibald McManus

Smout folded the letter and placed it back on
the table. An awkward hush hovered over the room.
Mr. Oxfam interrupted the silence with another plate
of shortbread.

"Well, he's gone to find your mum, so that's a
bit of good news," Bogey mumbled through the
fourth cookie he readily stuffed into his mouth. He
wasn't chancing it this time.

The five friends were meeting at Mr. Oxfam's
recently rebuilt bookshop. Flint the Cat was quite
content with his new surroundings. He had taken up

a comfortable residence in front of the fireplace which Mr. Oxfam had fitted with a more secure guard. He wasn't chancing it either.

"But he could have taken me with him. I could have helped," Smout moaned.

"Perhaps he thought you were safer here. Who knows what kind of people took your mother. I'm sure he'll find her, though," Emma assured him.

"Meanwhile, what do you say we find the treasure," Mad Dog suggested. He had actually gotten used to the nickname and decided he'd be alright if that's what his new friends called him. He'd actually even started being a bit nicer to the other kids at school.

"Do you really think he's left it?" Rory asked.

"Well, if there's a group of kids smart enough to find it it's got to be us. We could form our own treasure hunting club. Have regular meetings," Emma bubbled.

"Where would we meet?" Smout asked warily.

"I'm sure Mr. Oxfam wouldn't mind if we

met here."

"Not at all," Mr. Oxfam replied.

Rory grinned. "Come on, Smout. What do you say?"

Everyone sat on the edge of their seats, waiting to hear Smout's decision. After a thousand forevers, Smout tapped his chin.

"The club would need a name," he mused. He looked at the odd collection they made: the popular athlete; the tough bully; the class brain; the nose-picker; and the bug-eyed captain. An odd assortment of odds and ends. He looked up at the newly lettered window of Mr. Oxfam's shop. Gubbins Corner, it read. Smout's eyes lit up.

"How about 'The Gubbins Club'?"

EPILOGUE

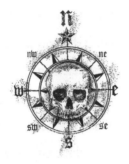

"Are you still writing? It's getting very late. The oil is getting low." Fanny smiled at her husband. She wasn't at all surprised to find him at the desk, scribbling away into the wee hours of the morning. His head was always filled with ideas and images that seemed to burn a hole in him until it flowed from his pen onto the paper. The image he had just been describing was particularly vivid. Fanny read it over his thin shoulder.

"'There are no stars as lovely as Edinburgh street-lamps.' Very pretty," she said. Her husband

MELINDA TALIANCICH FALGOUST

chuckled.

"Is that what you read there?" he asked an impish twinkle in his eye. Chuchu, the dog, stirred from his spot at the foot of young Lloyd's bed.

A smile came to his face. He was very fond of his stepson. Together they had already had grand adventures. He only hoped there would be many more. The young family had been squatting for weeks in the old abandoned mining town of Silverado. It was a curious arrangement and far from his native land of Edinburgh, but wherever Fanny and Lloyd were felt like home.

"What should I be reading, then? Suppose you tell me." Fanny smiled back.

"Now where's the adventure in that?" Robert Louis Stevenson stood and swept his wife into his arms. He carried her to bed, leaving his papers on the desk.

Before the oil in the lamp burned out, the wavering light danced across the words scrawled across the page. The phrase Fanny had so admired had been cleverly crafted, the letters arranged and rearranged many times over to form a lovely anagram. Unscrambled it read:

> *"So in the master's labor ever rests pyrate's golden haul."*